LITTLE BOY LOST

by

MARGHANITA LASKI

with a new afterword by

ANNE SEBBA

D1401583

PERSEPHONE BOOKS
LONDON

LITTLE BOY LOST

PART ONE
The Loss

CHAPTER ONE

It was on Christmas Day, 1943, that Hilary Wainwright learnt that his little son was lost.

* * *

Festooned with tinsel, glittering with gifts, the Christmas tree shone out of the darkness. At the tip of each branch the little pink candles wavered and glowed, and in their faint light Hilary watched the faces around him, the faces of his mother, his sister, his small nephew and niece. Now the children's eyes were entranced, his sister's boisterous jollity had softened into tenderness, and in the soft gleam of the candles it was possible to imagine that his mother's face offered him, not the cold hostility that he must always match with bitterness, but the comfort and love he had again come despairingly to seek.

And my own face? he wondered. Am I, too, transformed in this magical glow? If they looked at me now, would they see, not the stranger, the hated intellectual they must fearfully despise, but the jolly uncle, the loving brother, the dutiful son?

The little candles were quickly burning away. The glow was fading and already the children were straining forward, eager

to despoil the tree. One day the illusion will endure, thought Hilary, the day that John is with me at last, and between the two excited children his imagination inserted a third, the image of his own son.

'Lights on again!' ordered Mrs. Wainwright.

Now the illusion was shattered. The guttering candles were eclipsed by the electric light in the pink alabaster bowl, the tree an intruder among the walnut tables and the heavy velvet chairs. The children were squabbling over their presents – 'I wanted the Number Four set and Uncle Hilary's only given me the Number Two,' sulked Rodney, and Hilary, who had struggled among the Christmas crowds in the toyshops, buying with another child in his mind, thought that John would not have been so ungracious, and again longed passionately for the little boy he had never known.

'I must be taking my kids off home,' said Eileen at last. 'Nice to have seen you again, Hilary. Do you get any time to write your highbrow poetry in that hush-hush job?' She guffawed at her own question, struggling into her thick musquash coat. 'Come along, brats,' she called, and went out, driving her children before her.

'They're a dear little pair, aren't they?' said Mrs. Wainwright, coming back from the front door. 'I expect you notice a great change in them. Why, you haven't been over to see us for ages.' She stopped abruptly.

'What was the use?' said Hilary sombrely, and then he and his mother looked at each other in dismay.

She said hurriedly, 'I thought we wouldn't want much supper after that huge tea, so I told Annie to leave us some

sandwiches. It's all ready on the trolley if you'll go and bring it in.' They sat in armchairs on each side of the electric log-fire, and while they ate their sandwiches they cautiously agreed that Hilary was very lucky to have got Christmas leave and how nice it would be if Eileen's husband George could get a posting in England too.

Then, while the coffee was slowly filtering through the Cona, Mrs. Wainwright had the happy idea of bringing out the old snapshot album. 'This was the first photograph we ever had of you,' she said. 'You were just three weeks old,' and the memory of the total love she could give him in infancy enveloped them both in pleasing nostalgia. 'Here's a nice one of your father just before we got married,' she said, and there was the old doctor miraculously recognisable in the eager young man leaning against the sundial, unprescient of the death that would leave his wife and son locked in their bitter incessant strife. 'Oh, and here's the old house,' said Hilary, taking the album from her, and now the latent resentments began to stir, the irrational anger that his mother would not play the part he assigned to her – the dignified widow in the Queen Anne house by the cathedral close – but chose instead the bridge-parties and the brittle gossip of the London suburb. But this evening Mrs. Wainwright, instead of matching his instinctive hostility with her own, took the album from him and turned back the pages. 'Look!' she said, 'do you remember that holiday at Cliftonville?' and there was Hilary at five, neat grey shorts and jacket, neat brown shoes and tidy socks, round grey felt hat pulled over wide laughing eyes and a cheerful confident grin. His mother shot a quick

sidelong glance at him and then murmured, 'I wonder if little John looks like that?' 'Yes, I wonder,' said Hilary, wondering with all his heart, and his mother said tentatively, 'I do hope this horrible war will soon be over so that you can go and bring him home.'

Hilary tested the moment. Is it possible, he asked himself, that I was right to come after all? Is it possible that the years of angry misunderstanding could be erased, that she could give me now and for ever the comfort I so desperately need? Perhaps if I could only begin to tell her how much I long for my son – he was thinking; and then they heard the door-bell ring.

'Who can that be?' said Mrs. Wainwright irritably, and Hilary said, 'Annie's out, isn't she? I'll go,' and he got up and went to the front door.

The man who stood there was a stranger. He wore a shabby raincoat belted tightly round the waist and a knitted scarf wound tightly round his neck. He was about the same age as Hilary, and, like Hilary, tall and thin, but fair and with bright blue very tired eyes.

When Hilary opened the door he made a quick movement forward, almost as if he were going to stick his foot hurriedly in the opening, as if he were accustomed to forcing his way through doors that were shut again at the sight of him, though Hilary, realising this, thought in the same second that it was those who tried to shut him out who would be in the wrong. Because of this, he opened the front door wider and waited.

'*Vous êtes Hilary Wainwright?*' said the stranger, and at Hilary's surprise he continued quickly, and very quietly in

French, 'If you are alone, may I come in and talk to you? It is important, or I would not intrude.'

But now, despite his instinctive liking for the stranger, Hilary must be cautious. His job was genuinely secret and important. He said, 'Can you tell me something about your business? I'm really on leave, you know.'

The Frenchman smiled, relaxing surprisingly the tired vigilance of his face. He said, 'Your address was got for me by Brigadier X' and he mentioned the name of Hilary's brigadier. Then he added, 'You remember Jeanne? I was Jeanne's fiancé.'

Hilary started, and suddenly, uncontrollably shivered. Unthinkingly he had been convinced that the arrival of this Frenchman was in some way connected with his work, and the mention of his brigadier had confirmed him in this surmise. Now, though no credential had been given that could justifiably excuse him if he were wrong, he trusted this man. 'Come in,' he said, and his mother called from the sitting-room, 'Who is it, Hilary?'

He left the stranger in the hall and went hurriedly to the door. 'It's someone from my unit come to see me on business,' he said. 'May I take him into the dining-room?'

'Oh, dear,' said Mrs. Wainwright, 'can't they even leave you alone over Christmas? Yes, I suppose you can use the dining-room – it's been tidied.'

He closed the sitting-room door and led the stranger past it, into the dining-room. 'Take off your coat,' he said, 'I'll get a drink,' and he opened the sideboard cupboard and took out a bottle of beer and two glasses.

The Frenchman took off his coat and scarf and almost fell into the armchair at the head of the table. The skin over his face was tight with exhaustion, and as they talked in French his eyes kept falling shut and then opening too widely as if to hold them alert until this conversation was over.

He said, 'I had better tell you first that I have only got twenty-four hours in England, and no one except the people I have come to see is supposed to know I am here. My name, by the way, is Pierre Verdier, though you will please forget that till the war is over. It is outrageous that I have come to see you, entirely against discipline and my duty, but when I have finished you will understand why I have disregarded that and come. Only I must rely on you to tell no one that you have seen me now – your brigadier knows, but only he.'

Hilary said, 'If you are Jeanne's fiancé, I suppose I should have met you. But I don't remember you.'

'No, no,' said the Frenchman. 'We got engaged after the war started, and I think that after that you and I were never in Paris at the same time. Also, it was never an official engagement. But after France was defeated, I was still able to see Jeanne sometimes, and very occasionally I saw your wife.'

He paused and looked at Hilary, tensely interrogative, but Hilary was sitting stiffly on his chair, staring blankly in front of him. Pierre Verdier, fumbling for words, asked, 'Do you know – ? I am not the first to tell you?'

Hilary said harshly, 'I know that Lisa is dead. I had a letter from the Foreign Office.'

He opened his wallet, took out the letter and handed it to the man opposite. In stiff official phrases it had told Hilary

that the Foreign Office had heard, through unspecified sources, of the death of Lisa Wainwright at the hands of the Gestapo in Paris in December, 1942. It told her husband that no other information was available at present, but that if they heard anything more they would write again.

Pierre read the letter slowly and handed it back to Hilary. He asked, 'And did they write again?'

'Not exactly,' Hilary said. 'When I got this letter, I wrote to them and asked them if they knew anything about the baby, but I just got a brief note to say that they knew nothing, but again, that if they heard, they'd let me know. Since then, there's been nothing, except –' he broke off and swallowed to ease a mouth that had suddenly become painfully dry.

Pierre waited.

'I had a letter from Lisa,' Hilary said at last and with great difficulty. 'It was the third time I heard from her since I left her in Paris in 1940. Soon after I got back to England I had a Red Cross Post-Card – just five words, but I knew that she and the child were well. Then about three months later, I didn't have a letter, but an R.A.F. man came to see me. I was staying here with my mother then – I'd had my leg shot up getting out of France and it hadn't properly healed and I hadn't anywhere else to go.' He felt compelled to make the explanation, meaningless to a stranger. 'This R.A.F. man had been shot down in France and in the course of "being got out", he said, he'd spent a night at our – at Lisa's flat, and she'd asked him to come and see me. He wasn't much of a talker – he said she hadn't given him a note for me in case he was caught – but he said they were well. I saw his name in

a casualty list quite soon after. Then I heard nothing' – his voice that he had been carefully controlling rose and grew vehement – 'nothing, nothing at all until this letter came from the Foreign Office.'

Pierre said gently, 'And the last letter – the letter from Lisa?'

* * *

Sitting on the tapestry chair in his mother's dining-room, Hilary told over again in his mind the last letter from Lisa.

'Darling Hilary,' it began. These words were in English. The rest of the letter was written in French.

'I am sure that this letter will get to you, though it is the last thing I am sure about. I believe now that I have done you a great wrong. After you left us here in Paris, I should perhaps have thought of nothing but keeping ourselves safe for you. When I recovered, we could have got through to the unoccupied part and lived quietly and waited, though perhaps even there I might have been interned for being of Polish birth as much as for being married to an Englishman. One can't tell. At any rate, it seemed to me then that we should wait for you in our home and later that I should do the work I have been doing – I know that Ralph got back safely and so he will have been to see you and you will know what the work is. I believed that I must do this work, that I could do no less, and that the risks were risks we must all be ready to take if we are to deserve to survive. But now I find I am a coward and I am terrified for you and for our baby.

'It is just possible that it is still all right, but we don't think so. We think they have found us out and this is the end, and yet I can't go, can't try to get away, because, if it is all right, to go would be to admit too much. I have sent John to Jeanne. She is not implicated in this work I am doing, and she will see that he is safe until this nightmare is over and you can come and fetch him.

'My dearest, I try to write calmly, and tell you what I must, but I am filled with agony and I cannot put it on paper. I am in agony in losing you for ever. We have been so happy, we could be so happy again. I look round the flat and there is Binkie sitting on the empty cot, one pink velvet ear up and one pink velvet ear down, and I remember how you won him for me at the fair at Carpentras, and it hurts too much even to write. Often, these years, I have lain alone in bed and thought of your uncle's farm and how we would live there one day, not only with our little son, but with the other children we always meant to have; and I would be a farmer's wife, and you would write your poems and then we would be old together.

'You know what I feel, what I want to say, about us. But you have never known our baby, and I dare not let this go unsaid. Hilary, you must come and save our baby. As soon as it is safe, you must come over and fetch him from Jeanne, and teach him English and make him your son. I can bear everything, even leaving you for ever, but I can't bear our baby being without us, without the love that only we can give him. Hilary, I can endure everything if my baby is safe.

L.'

* * *

11

Slowly Hilary unclenched his hands, and dragged his mind back to the reality of Pierre waiting, his hands clasped on the table.

'And the last letter?' Pierre was saying. 'The letter from Lisa?'

'It was queer how it arrived,' Hilary said. 'It was in an envelope with Lisa's writing on it, and an English stamp. She'd addressed it here and it was forwarded to me at my unit. It gave me an awful shock, seeing her writing and that English stamp. I even thought before I opened it that the Foreign Office had made a ghastly mistake and that she was alive and here. But of course when I read it I understood.'

'When was it written?' Pierre asked.

'She hadn't dated it,' Hilary replied, almost as if he were talking to himself. 'She must have written it just before they got her, and given it to someone she knew was going to England. She said that Jeanne had taken the boy.' He looked up and suddenly stared at Pierre, tensely questioning him.

'Yes,' said Pierre, 'that is why I am here.'

He paused a moment, his eyes closed. Then he opened them and said almost casually, 'I told you before that my duty forbade my coming. It also forbids, of course, my telling you what I shall have to tell you to make things clear, but that isn't important now.

'You know, of course, that Jeanne and Lisa were friends since they were at the Sorbonne together, so that naturally when I became engaged to Jeanne I often met Lisa. That was when she was expecting the baby and you were out at the

Front. It's funny we didn't meet then, but we never had leave at the same time.'

'But I do remember now,' Hilary said slowly, 'I remember Lisa telling me one day about you and Jeanne – but it was just a thing she said – I never thought about it.'

'Soon after the Armistice,' Pierre went on, 'Lisa became part of an organisation for helping British prisoners to escape. I know Jeanne thought she was wrong; but Lisa said she must do it, and in those days all that was left to us was to do what we thought we must. Jeanne was doing something different.' He stopped, and then said with a mirthless laugh, 'I am telling you so much, I might as well tell you everything. Jeanne was helping to run a clandestine newspaper.'

'And you?' Hilary asked.

'I was, and am, underground,' Pierre said drily. 'It was because of my work that it was still necessary sometimes to see Jeanne, and twice, very shortly in cafés, to see Lisa.'

Hilary could see that the telling of this was indescribably painful to Pierre, that he longed for nothing more but to finish with it, but still he must interrupt and demand, 'How did she look?'

Pierre said very gently and without strain, 'She looked beautiful, even more beautiful than she used to look before the baby was born. She was so small and slight that I think we were all more frightened for her than we were for any-one else, but she herself always looked calm and serene and unafraid. It always gives me pleasure to think of her with her straight gold hair and her blue eyes and the beautiful bones in her face.'

'Thank you,' said Hilary. 'I am sorry I interrupted. Will you go on?'

Pierre said, 'The last time I saw Jeanne was at her flat, the evening of the day that the Gestapo had taken Lisa away. Your son was asleep in the bedroom – Jeanne had taken him two days earlier. We had all thought that Jeanne was still safe, that it was only the escape organisation the Gestapo had found out about.'

This time Hilary could not interrupt to ask the question that trembled in the air.

'We talked a lot that evening,' Pierre said softly. 'Though we believed we were still safe, each meeting was perhaps a parting for ever, and all through this one there was a feeling we had come to an end. Jeanne was looking back over the work she had done as though it was all finished. She said that she thought she had been wrong, that we had all been deeply and fundamentally wrong. "We have thought for years in terms of movements and groups," she said, "never of individuals. We have accepted the judgment of groups and we have subordinated our morality to them." And she said, "I know now that that was wrong. The only good thing we can do, the only goodness we can be sure of, is our own goodness as individuals and the good that we can do individually. As groups we often do evil that good may come and very often the good does not come and all that is left is the evil we have pointlessly done."

'You will understand,' continued Pierre, 'that this was an impractically idealistic point of view in France at this time. Nearly all the work that I personally was doing was evil by

Jeanne's definition – spying and destruction and murder – and I believed, as we all did, that it was necessary and right, not of itself, of course, but because the end was good. So I argued with Jeanne, but she had changed completely – one could almost say that she had had a conversion. She said, "One can never be sure of the end, only of the means, and so we must be sure that the means are good. One can never be sure of the motives of anyone but oneself and those we can examine to ensure that they are pure. All that seems to be certain is that we should each do good where it is near to us, where we can see the end of it, and then we know that something positive has been done." Then she nodded at the room where the baby was and said, "That's why the thing that seems to me most important now is to keep Lisa's baby safe and give him back to his father. If I can do that, I know that I have done something that is actively, positively right."

'I said, "What about the newspaper, then?" and she replied, "The baby is more important." Again I argued, because to our movement the newspaper was very important indeed, and she said she had known many people die because of the newspaper and she knew that was bad. To keep the child alive and safe she knew was good, and that was what she was going to do.'

Pierre lifted his eyes and looked into Hilary's. 'I became very angry with her,' he said drearily. 'I told her she was a coward, that she was a traitor to France, a disgrace to all patriotic Frenchwomen. I quarrelled with her passionately and I flung myself out of the flat, intending – you know how it

is when one is in love – to go back the next evening and make it all up. But it was too late. The next day at noon the Gestapo came.

'They killed her, of course,' he said flatly. 'I had been taunting her with cowardice, but she died under torture sooner than give away a name. We had been wrong when we thought that the Gestapo had only been after the escape organisation; it turned out to be a very big round-up indeed, and I myself got away only by a series of miracles.'

Hilary managed to bring out in a whisper, 'But what about the boy?'

'I was able,' said Pierre, 'to see Jeanne's concierge the next evening before I had to double out of Paris. She said that Mademoiselle had been out in the morning, before *they* came, taking the little boy with her, and had come back without him. She thought that perhaps Mademoiselle had taken him to the curé on the corner of the Rue du Vaisseau. I asked her why Mademoiselle should have done that, but she suddenly shut up like a clam, said she'd probably made a mistake, and anyway it wasn't any business of hers. I hadn't time to investigate further. I had to get out of Paris very quickly and I haven't been there since.'

'When you were in Jeanne's flat that night,' Hilary asked very carefully, 'did you see the boy?'

'No,' said Pierre sadly, 'I didn't. He was asleep when I arrived, you see, and frankly, I thought only of seeing Jeanne. No, I've never seen the boy.'

'I only saw him once,' said Hilary, 'and that was the day after he was born.'

Pierre sat silent and exhausted, and Hilary knew instinctively that between the telling of this story and saying whatever else he had come to say, he must have a rest, a few moments to sit without having to speak. So Hilary began to talk himself to the silent apparently unresponsive Pierre. He told Pierre how just before the war had started, they had decided that Lisa should stay in the flat in St. Cloud while Hilary went to England to join up. 'We all thought the British would be fighting in France,' he said, and sure enough he was quickly sent back again, now, with his excellent French, as liaison officer to a French battalion stationed near Sedan, and able to wangle sufficient leave in Paris to make the period of the phony war seem a perfectly tolerable one. They were both delighted when they found that they were to have a baby in June. 'I think,' said Hilary, 'from the way everyone talks now, that we must have been the only people in Europe who didn't know what was going to happen.'

Shortly after the breakthrough, the battalion to which Hilary was attached had broken and disintegrated. The way through to the British Army in the north was closed. The only practical escape was by the south-west. Hilary decided to make a dash for Paris first. He arrived there a day before the Germans, the day after his son was born.

Lisa was lying there in the big double bed, very white and very weak. It had been a surprisingly difficult birth, said Jeanne, who was there looking after her, but then Lisa was so small – The doctor had wanted her to go to hospital, but she had refused in case Hilary should come. And now he had come and was sitting beside the bed holding her hand, while

large weak tears rolled slowly down her cheeks. 'You must go,' Jeanne had urged. 'The Germans will be here. You must go while there's still time,' and Hilary had cried desperately that they must wrap Lisa in a blanket, find a car, get her out to England and safety.

But Jeanne had said it was impossible, and the doctor, who came in then, had endorsed it. 'Madame would undoubtedly have a serious hæmorrhage,' he had protested. 'No, monsieur, it is best that you should go. After all, it will only be for a short time. General Weygand will undoubtedly hold on the Loire, and you and Madame will be reunited very very soon.'

So he had let them persuade him and he had gone. He had looked round the flat, noticing with surprise that Binkie, the bead-eyed pink plush dog, had been deposed from his familiar place on the mantelpiece and was now sitting in the unfamiliar wicker cradle at the foot of the big bed. He had tentatively pulled aside a corner of the pink blanket. 'Pink for boys in France,' Lisa had explained, 'blue is for girls, the colour of the Blessed Virgin's robe – and our baby is going to be a son –' and he had seen, almost without noticing, the little black-haired red-faced baby swaddled in his shawl. He had kissed Lisa's deep blue tear-smudged eyes and he had gone.

'So you see,' he said, 'I only saw the baby once.'

* * *

Pierre was slowly recovering from his lassitude. He had lifted his head again and his eyes were wide open and surprisingly bright. He seemed steadily to gather energy as he roused

himself for the climax of all he had come to say, the true purpose of his visit.

'I want you,' he said, 'to let me find your son for you.'

Hilary said, 'How?' but it was no more than an instinctive response and Pierre made no reply to it. He was talking eagerly now.

'You know as well as I do,' he said, 'that if there is ever to be any future at all for any of us, the Second Front will have to be opened, and that if all goes well, soon afterwards France will be free again. When that happens, I shall be back in Paris – until then, I have no other work to do. Now you have your own work. I do not know if it will take you to France – ?' he paused interrogatively, and Hilary shook his head. There was no reason why his work should take him away from his Nissen hut until the war ended. 'I certainly don't anticipate getting to France,' he said, and Pierre went on impatiently. 'Well, even if you do, you will not be placed as I should for making enquiries. People will have many strange feelings after France is freed and you, even though you have lived in France, are a foreigner. You might even be deliberately misled – our people have got used to doing that, these last years. But I am accustomed to asking questions and knowing or finding out if the answers are true. If anyone can find your son for you, I can.' He stopped, leaning forward, his eyes fixed intently, pleadingly on Hilary.

It was only then that Hilary fully realised that his son was lost. Since Lisa's death he had ceaselessly dreamed that he would one day find happiness with a child who was not yet an imagined person but only a surviving symbol of his and

19

Lisa's love. But there had seemed no need to open his heart to this token child, safe in France and unattainable; his deep unassuageable anguish could be all for Lisa.

But now this Frenchman came to tell Hilary that not only Lisa but his child, a real child, had been lost, that the pity and agony must be indefinitely extended, the happiness and comfort indefinitely postponed. With horror he discovered in himself only a deep wish to be spared this new phase of pain, discovered that he was saying to himself, If the boy's lost, then let that be an end to it. He could not endure to imagine the possible agonies of the lost child.

But still Pierre was staring at him with this queer longing in his eyes as though Hilary had something very precious to give him and Hilary felt this and so asked gently, 'Why do you want to do this so much?'

'Surely you can see,' Pierre answered, in a voice deliberately dry of emotion. 'I told you what Jeanne said about the boy, and how I laughed at her and quarrelled with her. I feel that she would forgive me – no, that is untrue, I know she has forgiven me – I mean that I should be able to forgive myself if I could do what she wished.'

'Do you mean,' Hilary asked, 'that you agree now with what she said?'

'No,' said Pierre wearily, 'I disagree profoundly. It is a doctrine for saints – or for women in time of peace. But because I disagree, it seems to me even more important to do this for her.'

'I see that,' agreed Hilary. To carry out someone else's beliefs as a scourge for having acted wrongly to them was a

form of relief that to him, too, seemed satisfactory. But Hilary could not relieve himself of his own burdens in that way. He had no burden of guilt for anything he had done in the past; that was all in the future from this moment when a standard of attainment was to be set up and every future action must pursue or destroy that aim.

He said, 'You must forgive me if I seem all muddled. You see, until you came, I didn't know the boy was lost, and I haven't quite taken it in yet. Do you think you have any chance of finding him? What do you think will have happened to him?'

Pierre relaxed again. His face was smooth and he looked almost calm now. He said, 'It may, of course, be perfectly simple to find him. There are many families who are taking in Jewish children and children whom the Germans would otherwise take away. It is probable that the curé, of whom the concierge spoke, is organising such arrangements, and in this case, of course, he will know where the boy is, and we should have only to go and fetch him.'

'That's the best possibility,' Hilary said grimly. 'What's the worst?'

'I don't know,' Pierre answered. 'I don't know. I cannot tell you how often I have tortured myself, wondering. If he should have fallen into the hands of the Germans – we know that many children they have packed naked into trains with quicklime on the floor, so that when these trains arrived at the gas chambers, it was quite economical, because nearly all the children were dead already. They have killed children at the Gestapo headquarters in Paris, throwing acid at their

naked bodies. I am told that you can see the marks of their agonised hands in the concrete of the walls where they clawed at it – first, it seems there are the big hands of men, high up on the wall, and then below them smaller hands which are the women's, probably Jeanne's and Lisa's among them, and then lower and lower, come the little marks of the hands of the children.'

'For Christ's sake,' Hilary shouted, 'shut up!'

'You are new to this,' Pierre said, almost coldly. 'That's why you find it unbearable. When you have been one of us for a bit longer, you will discover, as we do, that it is easier to let your imagination comprehend all possible horrors than to pretend to ignore them.'

'No!' cried Hilary.

'I assure you it's so,' said Pierre. 'Really, it is as true of mental pain as about physical things. I remember a man in hospital in Marseilles – his hand had been almost shot off and was putrefying. He used to lie there with his eyes shut, never looking at it, just lie there for hours rigid with repressing his desire to look. Then in the end the doctor, who was a wise old man, insisted that he should open his eyes and look at it. I can tell you it was a horrible sight, that hand, because I saw it. There were white worms – But after this man looked at it – and it was some time, mind you, before he could glance at it naturally, not just stare – then, it started to heal.'

Hilary listened to the words Pierre said without opening his comprehension to their meaning. When Pierre had finished, he asked, 'Are there any other possibilities? – about the boy, I mean?'

'Well, there's just one more thing that might have happened,' Pierre answered. 'We hear that the Germans are taking a certain number of children from all the occupied countries and bringing them up as Germans. They take them young, change their names, put them into German families. Of course, they're only taking fair children – good Nordic types.' He paused and looked questioningly at Hilary.

Hilary said, 'My boy was dark – at least he was when he was born.'

'Children change a lot,' Pierre said dubiously, 'and Lisa was very fair.'

After this they both sat silent for what seemed a very long time, a silence of relaxation and sympathy. At last Pierre, looking a little less tired now, stood up and said, 'I have been thinking about all this so much that you will forgive me if to save time I force on you the plans I have devised. In the first place I have arranged that you will be informed if I am killed; so, if you don't hear, you will know that when Paris is ours again, I shall be looking for the boy. I will write to you as soon after that as I can.' He held out his hand and Hilary held it for a minute, finding comfort in a dispassionate sympathy that radiated from Pierre towards him. It was in no sense feeling for Hilary that had brought Pierre here; it was only that Hilary was accidentally comprehended in Pierre's debt to himself, and the strong liking each at that moment felt for the other was something permanent and comfortingly different from the heart-tearing emotions which had brought them together.

* * *

Hilary came back into the sitting-room and his mother asked, 'Where's your friend? Don't you think it would have been polite to bring him in here for a minute and introduce him to me?'

'He had to hurry,' Hilary said, picking up a green china rabbit, glancing at it without curiosity, and putting it down again. His mother said sharply, 'Well, what did he want, that he had to come chasing after you on Christmas Day?'

'He came to tell me that John is lost,' said Hilary, staring at his mother, trembling with the intensity of his desire that she should miraculously change into the image who would comfort him, only comfort him.

'You mean – dead?' whispered Mrs. Wainwright.

Hilary still stared at her, searching her face. Then he said with despair, 'Yes – dead.'

PART TWO
The Search

CHAPTER TWO

In 1945, three years after the little boy was lost, his father came to France to look for him.

* * *

In the ramshackle bus outside the airport Hilary wondered what had become of that strange excitement, that queer uplifting of the heart which he had always felt before when he landed in France. How often in the past years of exclusion had he not longed, with a longing so intense as to be almost carnal, for France, its sun, its tree-lined roads, its unforgettable urban smell, its soft sweet air. *'De veoir France, que mon cueur amer doit,'* he repeated to himself as he had so often repeated it, but the words had lost their magic. This was not France as he remembered it, the bombed airport, the anonymous suburban road, the British army trucks drawn up beside him. The commercial traveller he had chatted with at the airport now climbed into the bus. It was clear that he would have liked to sit by Hilary, to continue the comforting English conversation in the alien country, but Hilary had misanthropically covered the seat beside him with his trench-coat, his bundle of books and journals. 'You got somewhere to

stay when we arrive?' the little man asked, pausing beside him, obviously hoping the seat would be cleared, the invitation extended, but Hilary said coldly, 'I believe a friend is meeting me,' and picked up one of his papers. He was starting afresh now, unwilling to carry on with him even the barest former contact, and disappointed the commercial traveller moved on.

I hope, Hilary thought anxiously, that Pierre will be there. This France was unfamiliar, almost hostile, and he felt isolated and alone. He remembered the excuses he had made when Pierre's first letter had arrived with its tentative almost wistful suggestion that Hilary should come and see him in Paris and hear his suggestions for the search. It would be impossible to get permission while he was still in the Army, he had written untruthfully; he had sent the results of the blood-test that Pierre had suggested might be helpful, had been unable to find the photograph of himself at the age of five that Pierre had asked for. To get this it would have been necessary to go to his mother, to explain away the lie he had told her, to listen to the reproaches, the suggestions, the surmises he had lied to avoid. It was nearly a year since Pierre had first written, and now Hilary had been demobilised for a week and his excuse no longer held good; and Pierre had lately written that he must come soon, if ever.

For he would never wish Pierre to know his deep unwillingness to undertake this search.

He said to himself, It's been so long now since the boy was lost. I've had over two years to make myself invulnerable to

emotion. I can do without comfort now. I am content to live in my memories. All that is important now is that no one should disturb my memories.

If only the boy were already found, he thought, if I were married to Joyce, if my life were established, my conscience quieted and the old enchantments finally dead. But to achieve this I must kill the enchantments, myself undergo the agony of their death which will be the final death of the happiness Lisa and I had together. I have no courage, I recoil from the pains of leaving the past behind. But Pierre must not know this.

It had started to rain in loose light gusts, beating in noisy clouds against the windows of the bus. It was cold. Hilary shivered and longed for the bus to start, cursing the formalities that had held them so long at Le Bourget, passing them one by one through an incompetent sieve of officialdom.

At last they were all in and the bus jerked off, down the road to Paris. Now a tentative excitement began to stir in him with each remembered landmark – the shabby noticeboard in the field by the aerodrome that still offered 'Baptêmes de l'Air', the wall with its huge white-painted announcement 'Défense d'afficher', ignoring change and conquest, still quoting the constitution of 1875 for its authority; women with black frocks, black slippers, black shawls over their straggling grey hair, still shuffled over the pavement, long loaves under their arms. Yes, it was familiar again – until the bus creaked past the bombed factory, the makeshift bridge, the shattered rusting locomotives, and the English in the bus shamefacedly whispered to each other, 'Do you think *we* did that?' and then

wondered if there could still be friendship between the destroyer and the destroyed.

On and on rolled the rattling bus, through the narrow shabby streets, between the grey shattered houses, past the crowded windows of the drapery shops, the empty butchers'. 'Yes, I remember this,' Hilary said now and again, 'we're nearly there.' But each time he was deceived; unfamiliarity succeeded the false recognition, and his constant expectation of its imminent ending made the journey, made Paris, that little closed capital, seem endless.

Not even when the bus at last pulled up at the office in the narrow street off the Boulevard des Italiens had he established any sure recognitions. Bewildered, he tumbled out with the others, looking for his luggage, looking for Pierre, shepherded by assiduous officials into the office, through the office, to the last check-up, the last controls, the first chance to speak French again in France, as he explained that his money consisted of one hundred English pounds, twenty thousand francs on a letter of credit.

Now it was all over and at last the officials left him with his luggage standing alone in the hall. 'Do you think we could share a taxi?' whispered the commercial traveller, obsequiously sidling up to him. 'I don't know,' said Hilary, his eyes feverishly searching the room, the glass doors, the street beyond. Then there was a hand on his shoulder and a voice calling his name and at last he and Pierre stood face to face again.

'This is really good,' said Pierre sincerely, and Hilary grasped his hand and knew, as he looked at him, that it was

true that it was really good, this meeting. Here was a relationship beyond doubt or analysis, a liking and affection that had nothing to do with the circumstances in which it had been born.

'I've got a *fiacre*,' said Pierre; 'have you much luggage?'

'No,' said Hilary, 'just this one case,' and now he could say good-bye kindly to the little commercial traveller as he picked up his zipped bag and followed Pierre out of the door.

Outside there was waiting an infinitely shabby travesty of a cab, tattered grey canvas hood drawn down over a dilapidated wooden body, pathetically thin horse with its head drooping in the shafts. 'Real taxis are almost impossible,' Pierre said apologetically as he pulled aside the canvas for Hilary to enter and then followed him in, 'I was lucky to get hold of this,' and Hilary, encircled by the queer smell of fusty horsehair, said, 'It's a terrifying conveyance. It ought to be travelling a fictional road to hell with a spectral coachman.'

'You'll find that, like all spectral coachmen, he demands a heavy toll,' said Pierre. 'I suppose you've heard about the cost of things in Paris?'

Hilary nodded and tried to peer under the flapping canvas. 'We've just crossed the Place de l'Opéra,' Pierre said, 'I've got you a room at the Louvre. I tried to get you into the Scribe, which has got real hot water, but, as you probably know, it's requisitioned by the Press, and I couldn't fix it. Rooms in Paris are almost impossible now.'

'Where are you living yourself?' Hilary asked, and Pierre answered vaguely, 'Nowhere, really. Just staying with friends

here and there,' and then they crossed the Place du Palais Royal and the cab drew up outside the hotel.

It's impossible, thought Hilary, crossing the hall, swept up in the lift, walking along the corridors, that I'm treading where the German conquerors have trod. The receptionist who so politely gave me my *fiche* to fill in – had he performed the same service for Germans, bowing without a trace of hate on his face, without hate even in his heart? Is it even possible that it is I, not the German, whom he hates?

He burst out to Pierre as soon as the porter had put down the bag and closed the door, 'Don't you wonder, with every stranger you meet, what he did under the Occupation?'

'Oh yes,' said Pierre promptly, 'but automatically now and without caring about the answer. I'm tired with "collaborationist" as a term of abuse; we each did under the Germans what we were capable of doing; what that was, was settled long before they arrived.'

Hilary walked to the window and pushed it open. The room seemed hot and stuffy and to his surprise he discovered that the central-heating radiator was burning hot. 'I thought you said there wasn't any hot water,' he commented, and Pierre said drily, 'This is just an odd way of using the little fuel we have. You'll find that the water in the bathroom is absolutely cold.'

'Queer,' said Hilary, and then, 'But at least the Occupation showed each man what he was capable of. Don't you think it was something to be able to find that out?'

'No, why?' said Pierre. 'Some found they were better than they thought, some worse. We are finding that out all the time in our everyday lives.'

'But we're not conscious of it all the time,' argued Hilary. For some reason, this point seemed of vital importance to him. 'Surely occupation, or battle, or something like that, brings the whole thing to an inescapable point – a sort of judgment by ordeal?'

'And you long for that,' Pierre said gently. Hilary convulsively shivered and was silent.

Pierre thought, It is not at all as he imagines it. Ordeals never turn out the way you expect them. Usually when the ones you are expecting finally arrive there is no question of decision at all, and the ordeals of decision turn up on quite other occasions. He glanced at Hilary's face, noticing the sudden whiteness around his mouth, and wondered, Is it possible that this search has become the ordeal by which his entire judgment of himself will be measured? I must find out if this is so, he thought, and then he smiled and asked, 'Did you get anything to eat on your journey? Are you very hungry?'

Hilary smiled too, but his was the sudden smile of relief of a man who finds a friend where he feared an enemy. 'As a matter of fact,' he said, 'I'm ravenous. What's the tea situation here?'

'Tea,' repeated Pierre. He clutched his head in mock bewilderment. 'I meant to be such a good host,' he said regretfully, 'and as soon as you arrive you have me at a loss. I know nothing about the tea situation.'

'What about Rumpelmayer's?' Hilary suggested tentatively. He added, 'I feel rather like a Rip van Winkle, saying that. Probably you're going to reply that you once met an old man who remembered where Rumpelmayer's once stood.'

'Well, let's go and find out,' Pierre said with decision.

* * *

On the steps of the hotel, Pierre said, 'I'm afraid it means walking, unless you'd like to take the Metro. There are only about two buses in Paris, as yet.'

'I want to walk,' Hilary said. Standing there, he was becoming slowly intoxicated again with Paris. 'Don't you see,' he added, 'I can't believe yet that this is true? I'm in Paris again and it smells the same. Come on, we'll walk.'

They started down the Rue St. Honoré, Hilary eager now and pressing ahead. 'The queer thing is,' he said after a while, 'how everything seems to have telescoped in my mind. I thought I remembered this street perfectly, and yet everything is four times as far as I'd imagined it. I'd have expected us to be at the Rue Royale by now, and yet we're not even at the Place Vendôme. Did you ever have that feeling?'

'No,' said Pierre. 'There was a game we used to play sometimes in the evenings in Algiers. We would pretend we were walking down the Boul' Mich', and see who could remember most accurately every shop, every little street. Or we would say stations on the Metro.' He was speaking now in a voice Hilary instinctively associated with that evening at his mother's, and he glanced sharply at Pierre, only realising at this moment how much he had changed. The fatigue, languor and pervading misery that had then hung over him were utterly dissipated. Even his voice had altered. It was only then, hearing a voice which was the same as the one he remembered, he noticed that here was another man, a man

who was strong and confident, and surely, Hilary thought in bewilderment, a man who was happy.

'This way,' said Pierre, as they turned down to the Rue de Rivoli, and there, just as Hilary remembered it, was Rumpelmayer's.

'You see,' Pierre said in mock despair, 'it's always the foreigners who teach one about one's own city,' and they pushed open the doors and walked in.

* * *

The waitress brought their food; some tea without milk or sugar, a few slices of dry toast, a dish of unnaturally pink jam. Hilary and Pierre smiled at each other. On such trivialities their sympathy was sufficiently complete to obviate the need for the one to apologise that the food in France was so bad, the other, that in England it was so much better. In the warmth engendered by that smile Hilary dared to ask, 'Well?' and then to add, in the silence that followed his query, 'What have you got to tell me?'

Pierre said very slowly, almost reluctantly, 'I have found a boy who may, I think, be yours.'

'Where is he?' Hilary asked harshly. The question was not the result of conscious thought; rather, it burst from his tenseness and was meaningless to himself.

'I had better tell you all about it,' said Pierre.

'I got back from North Africa about nine months ago,' he began, and then stopped; and then swept aside this beginning that might have been devised to introduce a long detailed saga. He said abruptly, 'There's a woman who knows

35

as much about it as anyone. When we've finished our tea I want to take you along to see her.'

'But look here,' said Hilary, 'you've got to tell me about it before you go dragging me off to some woman. I mean, it's not –' and he, too, stopped. 'Not fair' had been the phrase in his mind, but this had been too obviously infantile to bring out. He looked at Pierre, and then saw, with a sudden pity, that Pierre was rigid with apprehension. It did not occur to him that Pierre's apprehension was for himself, for his own reception of the story. For the moment he wondered if perhaps he was going to be told something unbearably horrible, but this was only momentary, and soon he said with a gentleness born directly of his love for Pierre, 'Please tell me all about it.'

Hilary's unconscious relaxation made it easier for Pierre. Now he could light a cigarette, puff the smoke slowly through his nostrils and then remark, almost casually, 'Do you remember my telling you about Jeanne's concierge who told me, that morning, that the boy might have been taken to the curé on the corner of the Rue du Vaisseau?'

Hilary nodded.

'She wouldn't say any more then,' Pierre went on, 'she was obviously frightened to death that she'd said that much. But when I started looking for the boy, she was, of course, one of the first people I went after.' He sighed. 'The whole of this search seems to have been cursed,' he said vehemently, forgetting his care for Hilary. Then he went on in a voice deliberately dry of feeling, 'The damned woman had gone to live with relations in the Puy-de-Dôme, and it was a long time

before I could go after her. I tried a lot of things in the meantime – organisations of one sort or another – but none of them seemed to lead to anything constructive.' He paused, thinking sombrely over some of those unconstructive trails.

'But the concierge?' prompted Hilary.

Pierre said, 'Now that the war was over, she was perfectly willing to talk. She was a good-hearted woman – I knew that already – Jeanne had often said so. The trouble was that she didn't know very much. Apparently the curé in question had once or twice been to see Jeanne at the *appartement*, and once, when he came out, some crony who was gossiping with her had seen him and told her that he was working with the underground, concealing Jewish children from the Gestapo. And somehow or other, because, of course, nobody had said anything to her, when she saw Jeanne take the child out, it came into her mind that he was being taken to this curé to be hidden.'

Hilary said thoughtfully, 'I wonder if this idea she had – about the curé and the Jewish children, I mean – was because my boy was dark. She wouldn't have been so likely to have had it, do you think, if she saw Jeanne with a flaxen child with blue eyes?'

'It's possible,' agreed Pierre, 'but, of course, she knew or guessed that Jeanne was working for the Resistance, and people in that position didn't have children to stay with them for fun. The very fact that Jeanne had a child with her, fair or dark, implied that it was a clandestine child, and that would have been quite enough to put the idea of the curé into her head.'

'Perhaps,' agreed Hilary. For the first time he began consciously to try to imagine the face of his unknown son, but he could see nothing but a blank oval under one of those grey felt hats that English boys wear on the beach. 'I suppose you went to the curé after that,' he said.

'The curé was dead,' Pierre said flatly. 'That was the next piece of bad luck. He had died about three weeks after Jeanne was arrested. No,' he said in answer to Hilary's questioning eyebrows, 'there doesn't seem to have been anything sinister about it. He was a very old man and he died peacefully in his sleep one night of sheer old age.'

'It may have been a peaceful end but it was a damned inopportune one,' commented Hilary.

'It was appallingly difficult to find out anything about him,' said Pierre. 'He'd retired from active work some twenty years earlier – he apparently had a little money of his own – and he lived alone in this shabby little house, preparing some major work of scholarship on some very minor point of doctrine. This much I was able to gather from the neighbours and from the doctor who attended him. But nowhere did there seem to be any evidence to connect him with the story that he had sheltered children from the Gestapo. Mind you,' said Pierre, as one judging a piece of work by the highest professional canons, 'if he really *had* sheltered children, there *shouldn't* have been any evidence he'd done so. He'd have been damned inefficient if there was.'

'Didn't he have a housekeeper or anything?' asked Hilary helpfully.

'No,' said Pierre, 'he didn't. He had a half-dotty girl who used to come in for a couple of hours a day. I saw her, but

she was quite unhelpful, practically imbecile, in fact. And, as she was only there in the morning, she knew nothing about anybody who might call at other times. The only thing she was certain of was that never, never had she seen a child about the place.' He beamed triumphantly at Hilary, presented him with the valley deep in the mountains, surrounded by a seemingly impregnable wall of rock that will yet, to the practised guide, reveal the pass to the next valley.

Hilary was finding this story as absorbing as any other adventure that war travellers had told to him, the stay-at-home. It was with real yet impersonal interest he asked, 'What did you do next?' intent to hear how the path had been discovered, the wall of rock surmounted.

Pierre said, 'I hung around the Rue du Vaisseau quite a bit, talking to anyone – the postman, the stationer, the man at the café – who might be able to tell me something about the old man's contacts. On the face of it, he hadn't got any. There was nothing at all to connect him with the story Jeanne's concierge had told me. And yet it was just that fact that made me persist, that convinced me, without any logic, that he was not only doing underground work, but was being extremely efficient at it.

'One day I was drinking in the café opposite the priest's house when the wife of the *patron* came up to me and said that Madame Thillot, who owned the greengrocer's shop next door, thought she knew something that might interest me. Of course, I'd told everybody I spoke to what I was after. I didn't want them suspicious or hostile, and in fact, as you'd expect, they became extremely sympathetic and anxious to help.'

This was distasteful to Hilary. He could not contemplate his esoteric agony becoming the object of vulgar commiseration. Pierre noticed some recoil, some slight withdrawal and went on quietly. 'We've got a lot to thank Madame Thillot for. She was the only person who made a constructive suggestion. She told me to go and ask Madame Quillebœuf in the Impasse de la Pompe.'

'And who was she?' asked Hilary.

But Pierre had indicated the path that must be taken. He would not reveal until the proper time the route it would take to wind between the cloud-covered peaks. He said, 'Madame Quillebœuf is the lady I am taking you to see. I don't want to tell you about her. I want you to approach her story without prejudice of any kind. She's expecting us. When you've finished your tea, we'll go.'

'I'm ready,' said Hilary. He wanted desperately to drain the whole story from Pierre, to have it filtered for him through Pierre's understanding. He dreaded this irrevocable progress that Pierre had planned towards the moment when at last a decision must be taken by himself.

CHAPTER THREE

Outside Rumpelmayer's, Hilary said, 'Is it too far to walk?'

'Not if you don't mind walking,' said Pierre doubtfully, and Hilary replied, 'On the contrary. You forget I've been shut up in an office for the past five years while you chaps have been tramping all over the world. Besides,' he added on an impulse, 'I'm really a countryman.'

'No, really?' said Pierre. 'Were you brought up in the country?'

'Actually I wasn't,' Hilary admitted, 'but my uncle – my father's brother – farmed nine hundred acres in Gloucestershire, and whenever they could persuade my mother to let me go, I went to stay with them there. My uncle died when I left Oxford and he bequeathed me the farm. I let it, of course, and I'm damned glad of the income; it means that I can afford to choose my jobs for their own interest, like this literary editorship I've just taken up, where the pay is insignificant. But Lisa and I had always meant to go and live on the farm in the end.'

'Ah,' said Pierre, as if with sudden understanding. 'I see it now.'

'What?' Hilary asked.

'I read a book of yours in Cairo,' said Pierre, striding along the pavement.

Hilary asked, as an author always must, 'Which one?'

'It was called *The Orient Pearl*,' Pierre replied, barbarously mispronouncing the English words. 'Mind you, I am not a literary man like you, not at all. I never read French poetry, let alone English. But I saw this book in a shop, and knowing that one day I would have to come and visit you, I was naturally curious. And I tell you truthfully, Hilary, it was the first modern poetry I have ever liked.'

'Why?' asked Hilary abruptly.

'It was so happy,' said Pierre. 'I like to imagine the English countryside as you described it. I can imagine nothing pleasanter than to enjoy the English countryside with the woman one loves. You made modern love seem an Arcadian idyll instead of the metropolitan business it usually is.'

'I wrote that book in the spring of 1939,' said Hilary savagely. 'I was very young then.' He reflected with bitter wonder on the imagination of this younger man who had managed to fuse the love he was then enjoying with the countryside that had never yet really been his. Even my love poetry, he thought, was founded on an illusion rather than on the reality of the life Lisa and I were having together.

Pierre was saying, 'When I read that book, I naturally formed a picture of you in my mind. I thought you would be square-shouldered instead of lean, fair instead of dark, ruddy instead of pale, and happy – I mean with the capacity for happiness –' He stopped, appalled at what he had said.

They walked along in silence, for Hilary, too, was appalled at Pierre's last remark. To have the capacity for happiness was,

presumably, to be able to envisage a future in which happiness could have its place. But Pierre found him with the opposite of that capacity. Did this mean that his face was turned only to the past, that the future was no more than the time he must pass through as it irrevocably dragged him further and further from the only happiness he knew or could ever know? Or was he, perhaps, facing the future indeed, but with the capacity only for misery?

Suppose the boy is really found, he said to himself in panic. Mayn't that still give me an opportunity for happiness?

Suddenly there flooded into his mind the first two lines of a poem. He repeated them again and again to himself with great satisfaction, trying the sound of each word, the stress of each syllable. They had crossed the river and he was searching for a third line and a fourth before he consciously realised that this poem was one of proud resignation.

Pierre said, 'The first poem in the book was very different wasn't it? Of course, it was the only one that was about France, so perhaps that was why I thought so. Where were you thinking of when you wrote it?'

'Cassis,' said Hilary. He explained, 'That was where I first met Lisa,' and they relapsed into silence, walking steadily along the Boulevard St. Germain. But Pierre's reference to the only poem in his book that was founded totally on experience had slipped Hilary back into recollection. I know it is not recollection, but anticipation that I should endure now, he told himself, but again he said, no, not to-day, I'll think about the other things later, some time later. For the moment I must still have my drug of remembered happiness, and he let his mind slip back to the spring at Cassis when he had first met Lisa.

* * *

It was Thomas who had taken him to Cassis. It had been Thomas who had persuaded him when they came down from Oxford that a year in Paris would widen their literary capacities beyond all measure. So they had taken a furnished studio at the top of a decaying house on the Ile de la Cité, Thomas occasionally writing art criticisms for a very few very precious English journals, and Hilary publishing poems that steadily enhanced the precocious reputation he had already made at Oxford. But new contacts were the principal interest and purpose of their days, and it was as a result of one of Thomas's new contacts that Hilary found himself at Cassis in the spring of 1938.

They were living with a Russian sculptor in a dilapidated villa beside the Mediterranean. It was this sculptor who introduced Hilary to Lisa, who was decorously staying with her two aunts, Mademoiselle Doria and Mademoiselle Nita, at the most reputable hotel in Cassis.

Both Hilary and Lisa fell in love the first time they met. Neither had any doubt but that they must marry and spend the rest of their lives together.

There were no difficulties in the way. Mademoiselle Doria and Mademoiselle Nita were both delighted that Lisa should marry an Englishman. When they had been girls in Poland, the English sporting gentleman had been the most chic conception imaginable, and as this had been, in those days, a part that Hilary frequently delighted to play, each side was enchanted with the other. The Mesdemoiselles Vorotsky were Lisa's only guardians, and the only near relations she had.

Her father and mother had been killed while imprudently trying to fulfil a round of country-house visits in Russia in 1917, and Lisa's aunts had managed to bring the child to Paris where they had all lived ever since.

So in the autumn of 1938 Hilary and Lisa had been married at the British Consulate in Paris, and the Mesdemoiselles Vorotsky had immediately left, brimful of ebullient enthusiasm, to live with Cousin Elena in Rio de Janeiro. 'Are they being tactful and leaving us to try out married life alone?' Hilary had asked Lisa. 'It seems so strange their going off so happily when they quite obviously adore you,' and Lisa had explained, 'No, they adored me when they had to take care of me, but they are never interested in anyone who can take care of themselves. Cousin Elena in Rio has just lost her husband and has a cataract on her eyes.' And so Lisa's aunts passed out of their lives, passed away so completely that Hilary had never even thought to write and tell them that Lisa, too, was now irrevocably lost.

* * *

No possible interpretation of carefully given directions could have enabled Hilary to find the Impasse de la Pompe by himself. After they had passed St. Sulpice, Pierre had led him through a network of narrow streets until at last they stood in a cobbled passage-way, barely wide enough for two men to stand abreast. For fifty yards it ran between high walls and then a high wall abruptly ended it. There seemed to be no doors in the walls and only bare trees could be seen above them.

'What an extraordinary place,' said Hilary, standing in the entrance and staring at the grass growing between the cobblestones. 'This isn't Paris – it's some shabby village away from all the *routes nationales*.' He added with a kind of delight, 'It's a splendidly romantic place to begin a search from.'

'It is, isn't it?' said Pierre, with the gratification we always feel when our friends appreciate the discoveries we have made first. 'We are in fact between the gardens of a group of houses in the streets all around. Originally they were all the town houses of rich aristocrats – some of them still are – but the others have fallen to being publishers' offices and such like; one of them is even a plasterer's establishment.'

'But where,' asked Hilary with mock seriousness, 'is the residence of Madame Quillebœuf?'

'You will see,' said Pierre, and led the way down the alley.

At its far end the alley widened into a tiny round *place* perhaps eight feet in diameter. On one side of it a dilapidated standpipe rose from the cobbles, the last relic of the pump that had given the alley its name. Opposite this in the wall, invisible until you came right up to it, was an ironwork gate, backed with a defensive sheet of rusty iron.

'Through here,' said Pierre, and led the way in.

They were facing a little oblong box of a stucco house. Its front door was set in the exact centre of its façade, and flanked by two long arched windows of surprisingly beautiful proportions. There were no other windows at all. The flaking dirty stucco with which the little box was faced had once been covered with a delicate green wooden trelliswork, but this had fallen away in many places and hung splintered to the

ground. Two scrawny brown chickens pecked around the doorstep.

Hilary stared at it, enchanted. 'Is it,' he asked, offering the word that had leapt into his mind, 'is it a pavilion?'

'You are right,' said Pierre, delighted at Hilary's pleasure. 'This was originally the garden pavilion of the house that is now, as I told you, a plasterer's establishment. He had no use for this pretty toy, and so he rented it to Madame Quillebœuf. Come and meet her.'

They walked up the little path, still edged with the broken remnants of cockleshell borders, and Pierre knocked at the door.

It was opened after a moment by an old woman so tall and square-shouldered that Hilary stared at her in amazement. She was obviously a peasant rather than a Parisian. Her lean brown face was etched in deeper brown wrinkles, her carpet-slippered feet stood firmly and squarely on her threshold as if prepared to bar the entrance to any unwelcome callers. But at the sight of Pierre her great hooked nose and nutcracker chin came together in a wide smile and in a hoarse voice she said, 'So you have come back with your friend, monsieur. Enter!' and she stood aside to let them pass in before her, and then shut the door quickly.

It seemed that the whole pavilion consisted only of this one room into which they had come. It was not an attractive room now; the walls were covered with a dark brown paper in a heavy cubist pattern, and such little furniture as there was, was dark, heavy, and cheaply over-ornate. At the back of the room one corner was curtained off with what looked

like a ragged white counterpane. Over all hung a dank un-
attractive smell that Hilary recognised without being able to
name. Madame Quillebœuf pulled up two chairs covered in
embossed green plush, set them round a little gimcrack table
for Hilary and Pierre, and then stood before them, her hands
loosely clasped across her black sateen apron.

'I wonder,' said Pierre in a voice that Hilary had not heard
before, a slow patient coaxing voice, 'I wonder, madame,
whether you would start by telling my friend how you first
came to know the curé.'

Hilary looked questioningly at Pierre as if to ask if this
was really necessary, and Pierre gave a very slight nod. 'I am
accustomed to asking questions,' Pierre had said in London;
perhaps he knew that Madame Quillebœuf would find her
story easier to tell if she started with what she knew to be
simple and true.

'It's getting on for fifty years now since I first met the curé,'
she was saying. 'I'd just been married – my husband was
gardener to Monsieur le Vicomte then. The curé came to the
village and Monsieur le Vicomte lost his money almost at
the same time. So then my husband worked for Monsieur
Baudouin, the farmer, and we both lived in the curé's house,
and for the next twenty-five years I was the curé's housekeeper and my husband did his bit of gardening in the
evenings.'

'Tell monsieur why you came to Paris,' said Pierre, in this
same gentle coaxing voice.

'Well, my husband had his trouble,' said Madame
Quillebœuf. 'It was just after the curé had retired to come to

Paris, and the schoolmaster wrote him a letter for me, asking for his advice. He was always kind, was monsieur le curé – he knew of this little house, which is so cheap, messieurs, it is unbelievable – and he suggested that we came here, so that I could earn money by doing washing and sewing. And so we manage well enough, messieurs, though of late years my hands have been too crippled for the sewing, which leaves only the washing, and with prices rising as they are, that is not much, you understand. Still it is better than being poor in Normandy, which is where my husband comes from, for there every woman does her washing for herself, unlike these Parisians.' She said the last words with an expression of sly contempt, and shot a quick glance at Hilary, as if looking to see whether he would share her humour.

So that was the strange unpleasant smell, thought Hilary, wash-day after wash-day for interminable years. He wondered what her husband's trouble was, but did not like to ask. He was content to leave to Pierre this questioning that would at some moment tell him something about his son. But he wanted to be responsive to the atmosphere he understood Pierre was trying to create, and so in reply to Madame Quillebœuf's glance he twisted his face into what felt to him a wholly artificial grin.

But Pierre seemed content, for he too was reproducing Madame Quillebœuf's sly glee. 'Your washing turned out very helpful to a lot of Parisians during the Occupation,' he said with a wealth of meaningful innuendo.

'That it did,' said Madame Quillebœuf, 'that it did,' and she put her hands flatly on her knees as she bent forward and cackled vehemently, delighting in the shared joke.

'But monsieur doesn't know anything about this,' said Pierre, turning to Hilary as if he had just remembered him. 'Won't you tell him, madame, what you used to do with your washing during the Occupation?'

'I always did monsieur le curé's washing for him, ever since I came to Paris,' said Madame Quillebœuf. 'He couldn't pay me for it, of course, but it was only a little bit, and one doesn't entirely lack gratitude. Every week I'd go to his house with my big basket, after I'd called on all my other clients around the Rue du Vaisseau, and he'd always have a glass of wine waiting for me and a kind word about my old man. Then I'd stuff his bit of washing into my basket and take it up, and off I'd go until the next week.

'Well, messieurs, it went on like this year after year. Regular as clockwork, every Tuesday at about five o'clock – it might be a little more, it might be a little less – I'd go with my big basket to the curé's house. And then one Tuesday, just after the Boches came to Paris, monsieur le curé had a very different kind of washing waiting for me.'

She stopped to offer Pierre the questioning beginning of a smile, and he, responding, gave a hearty and encouraging laugh.

For the first time Madame Quillebœuf addressed Hilary directly. 'You wouldn't believe, monsieur, what was the washing monsieur le curé had waiting for me *that* Tuesday.' Hilary, understanding now that a responsive audience was the encouragement the old lady needed, shook his head with an expression of unfeigned bewilderment. 'It was a little boy,' said Madame Quillebœuf triumphantly, 'a little boy in a white

nightgown with lace on it, fast asleep in the big cupboard under the bookcase.'

Startled, Hilary glanced sharply at Pierre who almost imperceptibly shook his head. 'Wait,' said his lips, while his face quickly assumed the expression of rapt incredulity that the storyteller's dramatic pause demanded.

'Well, that's what it was,' she said, satisfied. 'A little boy with golden curls all over his head, just about two years old and looking like one of God's angels as he lay there. "Madame," said monsieur to me, "if you and I don't save that child, those accursed devils are going to kill him." And I said, "No, mon père, no one, not even a German, would kill a little child like that," because this was in the very first days after they had come, and we did not know then what they were capable of doing. But monsieur le curé assured me most solemnly that they would surely kill the child if they caught him, because of the good man that was his father, and so at last I said, "Well, mon père, and what is it that I can do to save him?" "You can take him home in your basket under the washing," said monsieur le curé, "and keep him safe until I can send someone to fetch him," "And what if he wakes up and cries on the way like a little sucking-pig?" I asked. "I've given him something that will make him sleep till midnight," said monsieur le curé. "And what if these swine should come and search my house to see if I'm hiding this or that?" I said. "Then there is living in your house yourself and your husband and the son of your widowed son in Algeria," said monsieur le curé, knowing well that our dear Isidor, who was dead these fifteen years, had been a bus driver for

51

the Compagnie Générale Transatlantique over there.' She stopped for breath.

'That was very practical of you, to think of all the difficulties before you acted,' said Pierre softly.

'Me, I am nothing if not practical,' said Madame Quillebœuf with a proper pride, 'practical and discreet, which is why monsieur le curé chose me for this difficult and dangerous work.'

'Well,' she continued, 'I took the little boy home with me, and for three days he lived with us, wearing only his little white nightgown, for I had no other clothes to put on him. But monsieur le curé was a wonderful man: he thought of everything. On the evening of the third day (which would make it – let me see – the Thursday) a young man came to my door just after dark. "Madame," he says, "I've come to see if you'll do my mother-in-law's washing for her," and do you know, messieurs, that was just what monsieur le curé told me he'd say. Then I was to say, "And where does your mother-in-law live?" – and so I said that, and he replied, just as he should, "Only five minutes walk from the Orphelinat at Auteuil." Each time someone came for the children – for it was not always the same young man who came – these very words were said. Then this young man, he pulled out of his overcoat pockets a little pair of trousers and a shirt and some sandals, and we put them on the child and told him he was going to his mummy, and off he went, as happy as the day was long.'

'And was he going to his mother?' asked Hilary.

'Oh, no,' said madame. 'His mother had already been killed. We only told him that to keep him quiet on the way.'

'It was well thought of,' said Pierre hurriedly, frowning at Hilary's look of outraged disapproval.

'That is what we always told them when they were fetched,' said madame, pleased. 'They were always good and quiet if they were told they were going to maman.'

'And where *did* they go?' Hilary asked.

'I do not know,' said madame emphatically, 'and I did not ask. The less one knew about other people's business the better. It is to be hoped that they went into good Catholic homes, for many of those who came in my big basket were little Israelites.'

What an outrageous woman this is, said Hilary to himself with unwilling admiration. He found nothing more difficult than to assess a character in whom attributes for good and evil were equally apparent; he allowed, if a little grudgingly, that the good might have a few small vices and the evil some little virtues, and it was his inability to set his own personality on one side or the other of this moral line that constantly disconcerted him.

Pierre was saying, 'Monsieur would like to hear about the last child of all.'

Hilary drew in his breath sharply and waited.

'Ah,' said madame softly and with infinite tenderness, '– my little Boubou.'

Hilary asked quickly, 'Was that his name?'

'That was what I called him,' said madame. 'His real name I never knew for no one ever told it to me. Boubou was what I used to call my own Isidor when he was just such a little scrap.'

She can't be talking of my child, Hilary said to himself. No child of mine could ever have reminded this grenadier of her

Isidor. He did not realise that for the first time he had felt his unknown child to be not a symbol but a person who must be protected against potentially hostile criticism.

'Tell monsieur how Boubou first came to you,' said Pierre.

'Why,' said madame, 'he came just like all the others, popped in my big basket of washing and fast asleep. There wasn't anything different about it. I just took him home with me, like all the others, and in the morning when he woke up, he said, "Where's maman?" just as they all did, and I told him maman was going to fetch him soon, like I always did, and he was as good as gold. He'd sit quiet and watch my old man for hours.'

'Why?' burst from Hilary with uncontrollable curiosity.

'Just look for yourself, monsieur,' said madame, and she strode over to the hanging white counterpane in the corner and jerked it aside.

Behind it, on a big brass bedstead, lay an old man. His hair and beard were white, his skin was grotesquely white and his open eyes stared vacantly into some indefinable distance. He lay absolutely still. Nothing about him moved save for a large bubble of saliva that, while they watched, formed slowly in one corner of his mouth, burst into dribble and fell over his chin as a new bubble slowly took shape.

'Yes, he'd sit on the bed beside him and watch him for hours,' said madame with a pride in her voice that seemed equally divided between her husband and the little boy.

Hilary felt sick. The sight of the flaccid face repelled him. He said, 'How long has he been like this?'

'Four years,' said madame stolidly, letting the counterpane fall. They came back to their chairs again. 'Before that, it was only one side that was paralysed. He was no good for digging or anything like that, of course, but still he could do little jobs around the house, feeding the chickens and this and that. But since he had his last stroke, he's been like you see him now. There's not much anyone can do for him now but feed him and keep him clean.'

Hilary, picturing these duties, felt his nausea grow. The enchanting little hidden house had become fetid and disgusting to him, and he longed to leave it and with it all the business that had brought him there. His sickness was so physical that he must choke it down and control it, fix his eyes desperately on Pierre who was saying quite casually, 'It was lucky that the little Boubou was so easily amused since you had him so long.'

'But never did I expect it!' said madame dramatically. 'Always the children had been fetched away before a week, sometimes indeed that very same evening, sometimes not for three or four days, but always before the following Tuesday. I didn't know what to think.

'Then the next Tuesday – just before Christmas it was – I go off with my big basket to the Rue du Vaisseau and they tell me that monsieur le curé is dead. Died in his sleep, he had, the very day after I'd taken my little Boubou home. Well, I didn't know what to do. I just came home with my basket again and waited for someone to come to the door and ask me to do his mother-in-law's washing.

'Messieurs, it was two weeks, three weeks, a month and still

no one came, and all the time I was getting fonder and fonder of that baby. I'd told him I was his granny, who was looking after him while maman was away, and "Grandmaman" was what he used to call me. I even used to pretend to myself that he was really the son of my Isidor – who, as the good God knows, had never married – and to hope that the knock at the door would never come.'

She paused and then lifted a corner of her black apron and one after another wiped away the tears that were welling in her tired red eyes. Hilary murmured to Pierre across the table, 'I suppose the old man had died before he could give any further instructions.' 'One would imagine so,' said Pierre softly, and then both waited for the old woman to speak again.

'It couldn't go on,' she said in a flat voice. 'After two months I could see that clearly. I couldn't keep the baby like a prisoner in this room all his life, never even letting him outside the door in case someone should hear him calling. Besides, I couldn't afford it. There was hardly any work in those days, and a baby must have milk, butter, good red meat, and what those would cost in the black market I couldn't imagine. And then he would grow. He would grow out of his clothes and new ones would not come out of the air. I would sit here at this very table, night after night, trying to think of ways to keep him and I couldn't find any.'

Hilary was forming in his mind a picture of the tired old woman bent over the table, desperately trying to think of ways to accomplish her impossible heart's desire, while the old man lay on the brass bed and the child – 'Where did the child sleep?' he asked suddenly.

'Why, over there with us,' said madame, in surprise, pointing to the dingy counterpane. 'Where else would you have him sleep? We kept each other warm.'

'Oh, God,' said Hilary under his breath, pity and disgust both struggling to assert themselves in the picture he was imagining.

Pierre said, 'It is indeed a problem when children grow out of their clothes. How was the little Boubou dressed, madame, when he came to you?'

'Ah,' said madame, 'you could see that here was a child that had been loved. The beautiful stitching on his little blouse – all hand smocked, it was – and a little pale blue knitted pullover on the top of it. And little woollen knickerbockers and little silk socks! Mind you, they were all dirty and creased when he came to me, but a washerwoman knows good quality and hand-stitching when she sees it.'

'Did he have an overcoat?' asked Pierre.

Madame Quillebœuf shook her head. 'No, he didn't,' she answered. 'To tell you the truth, I wondered about that myself, it being December when I first saw him, but then I said to myself, well, he'll be warm under all that washing and it's only for a day or two, because that's what I believed then, you understand. And monsieur le curé was looking so pale and worried I didn't like to bother him about it, though I didn't think then that it was the shadow of death he was feeling on him.'

Pierre sighed. 'And so after Boubou had been with you for a couple of months –' he prompted.

'I couldn't go on,' said madame with finality. 'Whichever way I looked at it, that was the conclusion I came to. Somehow or other my Boubou had to find a good home.'

In the infinitesimal pause before her next sentence, an imaginary saga raced through Hilary's mind. Among her clients Madame Quillebœuf knew a rich woman who had just lost her only son; she had taken the little Boubou, she was surrounding him with every loving attention, it would be cruelty to take him from her. . . .

'And at last I thought,' said madame, 'of the orphanage in the town of A —— where I was born.'

Pierre looked sharply and apprehensively at Hilary who, though not himself conscious of any change in his attitude, had suddenly stiffened in his chair.

Madame said, 'At once I knew that this was a good plan. But it could not be acted upon at once. Much had to be done first.

'There was the question of the fare. With rich people such a thing is easy. One takes out one's purse, one says, "How much?" and one puts down the money. With us, it is different. There are two places for every sou, and not for years has there been a chance to put anything away.

'At last I sold the clock. It was an act of charity. I do not regret it.

'Then there was the question of the child's clothes. Not only must he have a coat for the cold March winds, but how should I appear on the train if underneath his coat people saw that he was dressed like the children of the rich? At last I decided what to do. I put him to bed one night in an old

shirt of my husband's and then I washed and mended and ironed every stitch he had on. Mind you, he'd been wearing those same clothes for goodness knows how long now. I can't say they were in the condition they were when he came to me. But I did the best I could with them and in the morning I took them and I sold them.'

She stared at Hilary with a look of defiance that he could not interpret. Pierre seemed to understand. He said gently, 'I am sure, madame, that if the child's relations are ever found, they will say you were perfectly right to sell the clothes.'

'Well,' she said, a little relaxed but still on the defensive, 'that's what I did. I sold the clothes and I bought instead what was suitable for a child of the people. They were not new: I cannot pretend that they were. But there was all that was necessary – and you should have seen how proud he was when he put them on.

'The next morning we went to the station very very early, before the neighbours were about. I didn't like leaving my old man for a whole day – I'd never done such a thing before – but there was no help for it, and fortunately he was all right, though of course it meant a lot more work when I got home. I had a hard job persuading the Mother Superior to take the boy, but in the end she saw how it was. "Come and see him whenever you like," she said when I was going, but of course there's never been the money for *that*. Three years ago, it was –' she broke off and stood still, her mouth set in a rigid grimace of pain.

Hilary found himself saying, 'Madame, I do not know yet if the child you have told us about is the one I seek, but will

you allow me, on behalf of that child's parents, at least to repay you for the money you expended on his behalf?' Then he stopped, appalled at himself. He had spoken with a spontaneous impulse of gratitude and consolation, but had he, in offering to repay what had been freely given destroyed the beauty of the gift?

But Madame Quillebœuf did not see it like that. Her mouth relaxed and she said, 'Monsieur is too kind. I cannot deny that sometimes I hoped that perhaps one day –' and then, almost wolfishly, 'I cannot tell you how much I have need of money.'

Hurriedly Hilary took out his wallet, pulled out a note for a thousand francs and looked dubiously at Pierre who nodded vehemently. Hilary handed the note to the old woman who slipped it rapidly into a pocket under her apron and said solemnly, 'The good God will bless you, monsieur.'

Pierre whispered, 'Is there anything you'd like to ask her before we go?'

Hilary swallowed, and articulating carefully asked, 'Did he – did the boy ever say anything about his home – about his mother?'

The old woman thought for a minute. 'Of course, I didn't have much time to talk to him,' she said at last, 'and then there were so many children – sometimes I muddle up what one said and what the other said. You could see that Boubou was nicely brought up – he ate with his mouth shut, and once, I remember, I said, "Wipe your nose," and he said, "I haven't got a handkerchief."' She smiled at the recollection. 'Yes,' she repeated, 'that's what he said – "I haven't got a handkerchief."'

Pierre said under his breath, 'I don't think you'll get any more out of her. I've tried this line before, but there's nothing useful she remembers.'

He rose to his feet, made a formal speech of thanks to the old lady for her kindness in receiving them, and Hilary echoed him as best he could. At last they were out of the dilapidated pavilion, out of the little hidden alley-way, and in the noisy street again.

'And now,' said Pierre gaily, 'what about a drink?'

CHAPTER FOUR

Hilary said, 'That's a good idea, do you know somewhere quiet – I mean, somewhere where we can discuss things?'

'We can do all that later on,' said Pierre, urging Hilary forwards. 'But meanwhile I'd like to take you to a little bar I know. Some friends of mine often drop in there, and there are one or two I'd like you to meet.'

Hilary, bewildered, let Pierre lead him on. Surely, he was saying to himself, it would be better to have this thing out now, when we're all keyed up to it. He couldn't understand Pierre's sudden change of attitude, the cautious tenderness he had shown to Madame Quillebœuf suddenly superseded by this ebullient gaiety. For the first time since they met he felt himself wholly out of sympathy with Pierre.

But ten minutes later, drinking a Pernod in the little bar by Saint Sulpice, he had forgotten all about Madame Quillebœuf and her tattered doll's house. Pierre's friends were already there when they arrived. There was Edouard Renier who edited one of the more reputable of the innumerable literary monthlies. There was a short square woman with a strong restless face, who had been, Pierre said, devotedly happy in the Resistance movement and was now idle and lost. There

was an aristocratic young man who was a research chemist and an untidy black-haired creature who wrote political leaders for a left-wing daily.

With these people Hilary felt instantly and happily at home. These people were his friends, his chosen companions. Wherever in the world he happened to be, such a group would sooner or later be found and then he would be with his familiars. All these people would given the opportunity of choice, have the same sort of homes; you could go into a room in Prague or Budapest, Paris or London, and looking round at the pale-tinted walls, the heavy woven curtains, the big shabby armchair, the amusing piece of china on the shelf, you would know that this room belonged to a European intellectual of a certain generation, holding certain recognisable views. In each of these rooms the open light-wood bookcases would contain the same books; and, because of this, a whole conversational range of shared interests existed between members of this group as soon as they met together. They had no need to discuss the weather, to search laboriously for common acquaintances or pull out photographs of their children; once recognition had been established, there were no barriers.

Pierre's friends had all heard of Hilary. They were glad to meet him – 'at last' they said, as if he were the long-talked-of friend of some common acquaintance. There were questions they wanted to ask him, and the questions were informed and interesting ones on which his opinion could be of constructive value. There were questions, too, that Hilary wanted to ask, and these were the people who could offer him the opinions

which were the answers he required. And when, at last, Pierre took Hilary off to have dinner, Edouard Renier and the woman whom everyone called Bobby went with them.

They dined at a small dark dingy restaurant nearby, run – and this answer was becoming monotonous when Pierre talked of his acquaintances – by a member of the Resistance. The tables were covered with stained American cloth, the chairs were of hard brown wood; no attempt had been made to make this restaurant inviting to the casual diner who might hopefully open the door and look in.

But in this little shabby room Hilary had two hours of happiness greater than he had known since he had left Lisa behind in Paris.

To start with, the food was unbelievably luxurious. There was white bread; there were huge red steaks an inch thick, dabs of butter melting on top of them. There were meringues filled with whipped cream; there was a ripe Brie, a perfect claret, a suave Armagnac. Once – but so long ago ! – Hilary had understood food. He had treated his palate as a precious instrument of pleasure, and indulged it with esoteric knowledge. But all this was so far away that his consciousness had forgotten its sensations. For so many years now meals had been dull, methodical exercises less pleasurable, in terms of real pleasure, than the movements of the bowel that were their necessary complements.

And so it happened that the re-awakening of the taste-buds he had so completely forgotten simultaneously awakened in Hilary a sensuous memory of past pleasures. He remembered the smell of the hot Provençal grass, of

expensively perfumed women in good restaurants, of the resinous wine he had drunk in Greece. He remembered the sound of the cicadas on hot evenings in the South, the gipsy music he had heard on the Hortobagy, the roar of voices in the Italian market-place. He saw with vivid reality the sun shining on the black French roads, creating the mirage of shining water on the surface, the illumined blue sky behind the jagged line of high mountains. He forgot that in the past when he had had those things he had also had youth and freedom and a pre-war world; he knew only that the life before him suddenly held possibilities of pleasure that he had, when envisaging it, completely ignored.

Over the coffee and brandy the talk became practical. Would Hilary write an article, Edouard Renier asked, on the work of the émigré English poets during the war? Would he come later and give some lectures on English literature? His name was well known among the younger writers of France; Renier could promise him large interested audiences. And Hilary, in his turn, suggested that Renier should send him some articles on French collaborationist writers. They talked of painters in France and England, the woman Bobby now joining in with intelligent vivacity. They talked of the spontaneous renaissance of applied art in Italy, discussed its historical and sociological implications. And all this while Pierre sat back in his chair, silent and benevolently smiling. There seemed to be no need to drag him into the conversation. Once Hilary fleetingly thought, dear Pierre, he's no intellectual, this sort of conversation means nothing to him, and never appreciated, in his momentary contemptuous pity,

the discrimination that had led Pierre to choose among his acquaintances these two to dine with Hilary.

Then Hilary became aware that Renier and Bobby were lovers. He noticed Bobby's eyes devouring Renier's black-haired hands, Renier's full relaxed acceptance of her nearness to him. Gradually his unthinking delight in the evening faded into that nostalgic romantic sadness in which we can easily weep, not for ourselves and our immediate sorrow, but for the larger tragedy of ourselves in a tragic world.

'We must go,' said Pierre without explanation or excuse. He had become as sensitive to Hilary's moods as a mother to her only child. Outside the restaurant he said, 'I feel I've been thoughtless. Perhaps there are some old friends of your own you'd like to go and see?'

'No,' said Hilary abruptly. His life with Lisa in Paris had not included any French friends whom he might expect to find still, after war and occupation, inevitably established in their own homes. He had thought, when he lived here, that he had entered fully into France and the life of the French. Now he realised that all the people he had known were people like himself, Englishmen and Poles and Americans and German refugees, intellectual expatriates whom the war had blown away.

'Then we'll go and sit outside the Café de la Paix,' said Pierre with determination. 'You are a foreign tourist and I always do the correct thing with foreign tourists.'

It was a good choice. The crowds swirled and clattered by, the bearded man at the next table picked up a little blonde

prostitute, the two dark immaculately-groomed women played their mondaine parts with their two immaculate escorts. Hilary forgot his momentary wistfulness and looked about him with eager attention.

It was only then that Pierre asked, 'What did you think of Madame Quillebœuf's story?'

'I am accustomed to asking questions,' Pierre had said, but Hilary did not remember this. He did not realise that because of the evening Pierre had planned for him he had undergone a catharsis that now made it possible to discuss the matter without tenseness or a deep inhibited unwillingness to do so. He asked the question that had been puzzling him:

'Why were you so keen to know if the child had worn an overcoat?'

Pierre sighed. 'Jeanne's concierge had been able to describe in some detail the coat your boy was wearing when Jeanne took him away,' he said. 'If Madame Quillebœuf had seen the same coat, the evidence would have been conclusive.'

'And as it is?' Hilary asked.

'I think this is your son,' Pierre said firmly.

When they had left Madame Quillebœuf's house, Hilary had been convinced that the story he had been told about the little Boubou had been a story about his own child. Now intellectual objections were beginning to obscure his conviction. He said, 'There's no real evidence that he is.'

'No, there isn't,' Pierre agreed, 'but there is a very strong degree of probability. We know that Jeanne knew the curé. Presumably she knew that he had placed other children in safety, and it would have been the obvious thing for her to

turn to him when she realised that she could no longer keep the child safely herself, and that she probably had very little time left to make arrangements for him. The dates are about right; Madame Quillebœuf is a bit hazy as to the exact date when she actually took the child, but from what she says, it was a week or two before Christmas. Now Jeanne was arrested on December 10th, so, assuming that the child spent nearly a week with the curé before the old woman took him, that would be about right. And there's one more thing; I've had a blood-test done on the child and his blood is the same group as yours. I agree that isn't conclusive, but taken with all the rest, it's most suggestive.'

'There are a lot of gaps,' Hilary said obstinately. 'For instance, about this coat question. It was mid-winter, remember. Since we know that my child definitely had an overcoat when Jeanne took him off, why should the curé have let him go off in the cold without it?'

Pierre said, 'I can think of a lot of reasons. The curé may have thought that the coat could be identified by anyone who had seen Jeanne with the boy – as, indeed, it could have been if the Gestapo had been looking for the child. Or the child might have been out in the rain, and the coat be too wet to put on. Or, which is more likely, the child simply hadn't got the coat on when the curé drugged him to keep him quiet, and later, when Madame Quillebœuf came, the curé, being an old man, just forgot about it. Remember, the first child she took was wearing nothing but a nightgown, and appropriate clothes were sent when necessary when the children were fetched.'

'That's all quite plausible,' Hilary said grudgingly. Some impulse was now desperately driving him to fight against his original conviction that this was his son. 'The trouble is,' he said, 'that though this *might* be my child, it equally well might not. I can think of so many other possibilities. For instance, Madame Quillebœuf may not have been the curé's only contact for disposing of these children. And then we don't really know that Jeanne took my boy to the curé. She may have taken him somewhere quite different. The Gestapo may even have got him, and he might have died in one of those trains you were talking about or be a happy little Nordic boy in some German home. Have you,' he added aggressively, 'ever thought of that?'

Pierre said patiently, 'Of course I have. But if either of those things has happened, you will never know, and you will never find him. The only assumption on which we can work is that he did *not* fall into the hands of the Gestapo. Personally I am convinced that he didn't. Jeanne was entirely competent, and if she took the boy to safety, it would have been to real safety.'

'Still,' said Hilary, 'you can't be *sure*.'

'No,' said Pierre.

'Even if we assume that the boy is definitely in France,' Hilary argued, 'I don't want to go and claim this child and then have my own turn up somewhere quite different.'

'That won't happen,' Pierre said, 'I can assure you of that. Believe me, Hilary, if this child is not yours, you will never find your child.'

Not if I can help it, he added to himself. Not through him

69

would Hilary ever know of the boy who mouthed and whimpered in an asylum at Tours, who could well, for dates and blood-tests and all that was known of his history, be Hilary's son. Nor would he tell him of the little boy who was now the sole consolation of the parents near Lyons whose own two boys had been caught by the Gestapo and tortured before they died; if this little boy, who had come through channels so tortuous that no one could now retrace them, was indeed Hilary's son, then Hilary's son must remain for ever lost. Pierre saw in his mind the confidently happy face of the one child, the imbecile slobber of the other, and then shut them away. He genuinely believed that of all these children, the little Boubou was the most likely to be the one they were looking for.

'Have you yourself seen the child in question?' Hilary asked.

'No,' said Pierre, 'I haven't. I thought you would want us to go to A—— tomorrow.'

Hilary said, 'If only I could be *sure.*'

'I am convinced,' said Pierre, 'that the only way you can be sure is to go and see the boy for yourself. For one thing, I am a great believer in instinct. If this is really your son, I am sure that you will know it as soon as you set eyes on him. And even if instinct lets you down – as it tends to, when we become too civilised, too intellectual – there remains the possibility of conclusive evidence that only you can collect. You know your own family; you will perhaps notice that he has some mannerism peculiar to your mother, or looks just like the pictures of your uncle at the same age. And not only that; if

you get to know the child and talk to him a bit, you may be able to make him remember all sorts of things about his past life and surroundings, things that would be quite meaningless to anyone but you.'

'There's a lot in what you say,' Hilary agreed, 'though I rather doubt the last part of it. The boy was only two and a half when he was taken away, and now he must be well over five. I don't know a lot about small children, but I can't myself remember anything that happened before I was three.'

'But you're grown up,' Pierre argued, 'you don't know now what you remembered when you were five.'

'That's true,' Hilary said thoughtfully. It's possible, he conceded, that Pierre's right, that once I've seen this child I'll somehow know whether he's mine or not; and then fleetingly the thought crossed his mind, if Pierre's with me, I won't be able to reject the child. He looked up at Pierre with a new apprehension, realising that here might be the enemy after all.

'Tell me,' Pierre was saying in a changed voice, 'what are you going to do with the child if he's really yours? Have you got a home for him, or are you still living in your mess?'

'No, I was demobilised last week,' Hilary answered, 'but even so I don't quite know what I'd do with the child. At the moment I'm sharing a flat in a rather beautiful house off Regent's Park with Thomas – he's the friend I lived with in Paris before I married – but it's not the sort of place where one would want to keep a child.'

He recalled with pleasure the beautiful little Regency terrace house where they had found their flat, the books,

the gramophone records, the privacy and seclusion. Life in the flat would be safely unemotional, his relationship with Thomas having always remained on the placid level of respect for mutual achievement. It was unthinkable that a child should invade this refuge. 'Besides,' he added, 'there's no one to look after him.'

'What about your mother?' Pierre suggested. 'In my experience grandmothers are usually only too anxious to take care of their son's children.'

'I'm afraid that would hardly do,' Hilary said coldly. 'My mother and I don't get on well together.' He was deeply affronted by the suggestion. No child brought up by his mother could be the child with whom Hilary had once imagined that happiness might be possible. He shuddered, envisaging with entirely humourless horror the suburban net drawn close about his feet.

Pierre said, 'Forgive me, Hilary, if I'm intruding – but have you ever thought of getting married again?'

Hilary picked up the ashtray and carefully set it down again exactly half-way between their two glasses. He answered in a deliberately expressionless voice, 'I have,' and then a longing for consolation made him say in a voice half-eager, half-frightened, 'Do you mind if I tell you about it?'

'Please,' said Pierre.

'Her name's Joyce,' Hilary said. 'I met her during the war – she was P.A. to my commanding officer. She's been married before to some journalist fellow when she was very young, just after she left Oxford. I gather it didn't work out at all; anyway, she got divorced very soon after. She's twenty-eight.'

'What's she doing now?' Pierre asked. He guessed this was the right question about an Englishwoman who had been to Oxford and was now unmarried.

'She's in the B.B.C.,' Hilary said. 'Got a very good job.'

'And what's she like?' Pierre asked.

'She's a very nice girl,' Hilary said, between admiration and contempt. 'She's intelligent, well-educated, competent, good, kindly. She reads *The New Statesman* every week and takes an informed interest in politics. Also, she's in love with me.'

'But it all sounds admirable,' said Pierre, feeling in his heart an immeasurably deep relief. 'I should imagine you could have a very happy life with her.'

'That is what one would imagine, isn't it ?' agreed Hilary bitterly.

Pierre said sharply, 'Hilary, I tell you honestly that I don't understand. What is there in the prospect of marriage with this Joyce that seems so displeasing to you?'

Hilary again picked up the ashtray, tried it here, tried it there. Still playing with it, he said in a low voice, 'It's three years since you came to tell me that John was lost.'

He was silent for a minute and then, still looking down at the table, he whispered, 'Just before you came, I was longing for him. It was Christmas – do you remember? We'd had the tree and I'd been looking at it and wanting the boy – I can't tell you how much I was wanting him then.'

Now that he had started to explain, he could not stop. Even though he might be explaining, not to his friend but to his enemy, the words must gush out.

'It was twice,' he said, 'twice within a year. First Lisa was gone and that was agony – *you* know what agony that was,' he said accusingly, looking suddenly up at Pierre. Then again his eyes were on the ashtray he was pushing aimlessly around the table. 'After Lisa had gone,' he said, 'I could still believe that one day there would be some warmth and comfort again because the boy was still alive. He was mine and Lisa's, part of ourselves, something that was made from the only security I've ever known. Then you said that he was gone too, and there was nothing, no warmth, no love, nothing ahead at all.

'I've had three years,' he said with despair, 'three years to stop feeling anything. I couldn't do what you said – imagining how Lisa died, I mean – I couldn't think about it. I couldn't think about the boy being lost, how he'd wonder what had happened, how people might be cruel to him, how lonely he'd be –' He raised an anguished face to Pierre and pleaded, 'Pierre, I couldn't think about it. I don't want to think about it now.'

'But perhaps it is all over now,' Pierre said softly. 'Perhaps the boy is found.'

'It's too late,' Hilary said in a dead voice. 'I don't want to feel anything any more. Before I met Lisa, I had never felt anything like tenderness or love. My mother –' He broke off this sentence and started again. 'I thought that I never would be able to feel anything like that, and then I met Lisa and you know how happy we were, how perfect it was. But after you'd gone, I thought it would have been better never to have been happy, never to have felt love and tenderness and all those things, than to have known them and then lost them.'

Pierre said in the same soft voice, 'If the boy is found, those things will be found again too.'

'I don't want them,' Hilary cried harshly. Now he was saying much more than he had intended, but he could not stop himself. 'I can do without those things,' he cried. 'I couldn't endure being hurt again; I'd sooner feel nothing. I don't like children as such; they bore me. I used to think that a child of my own would make me happy, but I know that isn't true any more. I've got nothing to offer a child and I've got nothing to offer Joyce. I just want to be left alone so that I can't be hurt again.'

Pierre sighed, 'Poor little boy.'

Hilary slowly realised that the sympathy was not for himself but for the lost child. This was unendurable. Secretly he knew that he had let himself talk so that at the end Pierre's sympathy would be all his, and with the discovery that this was not so, his growing resentment against Pierre mounted into anger. Abruptly he demanded, 'Tell me how it is that *you* manage to seem so happy and so – so confident?'

Pierre was not introspective. He preferred to generalise about life rather than to particularise about himself. He said, lifting his eyebrows in surprise, 'Do I seem very happy and confident?'

'Yes,' said Hilary savagely, 'you do. And why you and not me? After all,' he fumbled with a phrase and then found one with delight, 'we've both been cuckolded by death.'

'Yes,' said Pierre, respecting and savouring the sentiment, 'we have.' He paused, and then offered, 'I imagine it isn't in my nature to live in the past.'

Hilary was compelled to continue his questioning. 'Have you fallen in love again?' he demanded.

'Oh, no,' said Pierre, 'that doesn't seem to be in my nature either. Mind you,' he added, 'I don't mean to suggest that I practise celibacy. No, it is simply that that part of my life seems no longer to hold the possibilities of emotional interest.'

Now Hilary deeply and jealously envied Pierre. Hilary had not himself practised celibacy. He had had the weekend leave with Rose, the local tart at the garrison town where he had once been sent on a course, the uneasy three months' relationship with Hedi, the little refugee from Vienna. But he had never been able casually and happily to sleep with a woman when he desired one. Despite his conscious determination to seek nothing but physical satisfaction, he was still unconsciously always looking for some indefinable transcendental comfort in the sexual relationship, and, never finding it, was always sexually disappointed and dissatisfied. He asked Pierre sharply and angrily, as if he would tear the answer from him, 'Then what *is* it that makes you happy?'

'I suppose,' said Pierre, 'it is because I've found something to live for.'

'And what is that?' Hilary demanded.

Pierre said, 'For the past five years I have never known whether I was a hero or a traitor. Now, I wish to be sure at least that I am a patriot. I have given myself to the service of General de Gaulle.'

With sharp relief Hilary allowed this single answer totally to destroy his sense of friendship and obligation towards Pierre.

He could let himself believe that he had been cheated and deceived. 'That Fascist' he said to himself, for in Hilary's credo General de Gaulle was a wrong man, irrevocably set on the wrong side of the moral line. No one, in the esoteric society to which he confined himself, could conceive of holding a different view. Since Pierre held this different view, then he must be outside this society and therefore unacceptable to Hilary. The sympathy that had flowed between them had sprung from false premises. Hilary's recognition of Pierre as the same kind of creature as himself had been irremediably wrong. With exaltation he told himself, I am free of Pierre. I can decide alone.

In that instant he cast out Pierre so totally that he could no longer even pay him the compliment of argument. Instead he said in a warmer voice than he had yet used, 'How very interesting' and then, with a yawn, 'Well, I think I'd better be getting back to the hotel now.'

Pierre had sensed Hilary's withdrawal without beginning to comprehend it. He said anxiously, 'The train for A—— leaves the Gare du Nord at half-past ten tomorrow morning.'

'Good,' said Hilary. They started to walk together down the Avenue de l'Opéra. Hilary said, 'By the way, what's the name of this orphanage?'

'Notre-Dame-de-la-Pitié,' Pierre answered, and Hilary questioned, 'I suppose the Mother Superior knows all about me?'

'Oh, yes,' said Pierre, happier now that he could instruct Hilary again. 'I wrote and told her all about you when I asked her to have the blood-test done. She's expecting us tomorrow.'

Hilary said with the most careful casualness, 'I wonder, old man, if you'd mind very much if I asked you to let me go alone?'

Pierre said emptily, 'Of course, if you wish it.' It was plain that he was bitterly, painfully disappointed.

Hilary now almost believed that he had cast Pierre away for a political principle of the highest morality. In telling Pierre some part of the truth, he could let himself think that he was uttering a kindly lie. He said, 'You know there's nothing I'd like better than to have you with me, but I don't quite feel it would be right. I respect your judgment so much that I'd be afraid of deferring to it, and in this particular case I feel it's vitally important that I should come to my decision without any outside influence. I've got to go through with this by myself,' and at a lower level of consciousness the thought burst through, 'I've got to be free to escape.'

'That is reasonable,' Pierre said hopelessly. 'I have no right to force you to undertake my own expiation.'

He was understanding too much. They had reached the hotel now and Hilary said hurriedly, 'Of course I'll let you know what happens.' 'Thank you,' said Pierre, and then persisted, as if he couldn't help himself, 'And if I can do anything more – if you should want me to come –.'

With that false warmth which was all he had left to offer, Hilary repeated, 'Of course.' He's a fascist, he reminded himself; to take him with me would be to contaminate my ordeal.

'Good-bye, then,' Pierre said sadly, and walked down the steps and away.

CHAPTER FIVE

Although the town of A—— was only fifty miles from Paris, the train had taken nearly four hours to get there. Crowded almost beyond capacity, it had crawled across the undulating plain of Northern France, slowed down almost to walking pace at each ramshackle temporary bridge, called at every little station, and periodically simply stopped for long intervals in the open fields without any apparent reason. At last, after half an hour's shunting and puffing through a landscape of slagheaps and bombed factories, it had left Hilary on the platform at A—— and jerked slowly away.

The station was on the very perimeter of the town. Carrying his bag, he walked away down the wide shabby boulevard facing him. The town of A—— was clearly one of those that had been grossly damaged in the first world war and rebuilt with that haphazard disregard for appearance so characteristic of modern France. Now a second war had come to shatter the grimy ironwork façade of the garage, pit with bullet-holes the walls of the gaudy scarlet-and-yellow brick villa. Overhead the wires of the tramlines hung in tangled confusion, and underfoot the tarmac was broken and pot-

holed. Most people were presumably relaxing after lunch, for the streets were almost empty.

Everywhere he looked he could see nothing but ugliness. No one had given to the first rebuilding of the town of A—— any other considerations than those of prestige and sheer utility. He came to a large square with a war memorial in the middle, a *poilu* thrusting with a bayonet on a ragged plinth of granite. He could see that he was still only on the outskirts, and he stopped a passer-by and asked, 'Where is the centre of the town?' The man jerked his thumb down a street, and Hilary, his bag noticeably heavier now, walked down it.

This street curved away so that only its beginning could be seen from the square. He rounded the curve, and then found a wilderness of desolation. Save for a roofless church higher for the contrast of emptiness, there was not a building standing for half a mile in every direction. Red bricks and grey bricks, roof tiles and stucco, reinforced concrete spouting thick rusty wires, all lay huddled in destruction. Nothing seemed to have been cleared away save what was necessary to allow a few tracks to pass through. It was ruin more complete and desolate than Hilary had ever seen.

He was stabbed with an impulse of deep pity. This town had always been ugly. Its life could never have been one that he himself would have wanted to share. Yet, where these ruins now stood, the people who were part of the nation he regarded as the most civilised in the world had led full satisfactory lives, eating with informed pleasure, arguing with informed logic, strolling up and down in the warm summer evenings, sitting at cafés and watching the promenade pass

by. Here housewives had made their purchases with that unconscious pleasure and pride that comes from the competent practice of a craft, prodding the cabbages to see what sort of hearts they'd made, testing each length of cloth, pulling the glove leather this way and that, purchasing by their own skill from shopkeepers who respected this quality in their customers. It seemed to Hilary that bomb damage in a French town was a greater tragedy than elsewhere because here the way of life destroyed was in complete antithesis to all that bombs were trying to achieve. He wanted himself to pick up the shovel, to start with his own physical exertions clearing up this mess and wiping out this loss.

His conscience said, 'But you can. There is the child to find and save.'

He walked quickly among the ruins, looking ahead to where buildings still stood. He came to the shattered church and here a man was working with a wheelbarrow, coming out through the big doors with the barrow full of fragments of bright blue and gold plaster. Hilary walked up to him and asked, 'Is there still an hotel in the town?'

The man said, 'You may well ask.' He pointed to a pile of debris opposite the church and said, 'That was the Lion d'Or.' He pointed in another direction and said, 'That was the Hôtel de la Cygne.' Then he picked up his barrow again and nodded his head down a little cleared track. 'Down there,' he said, 'you will find the Hôtel d'Angleterre,' and then he walked away.

The rubble abruptly ended and the buildings started again. This was an older part of the town and it had evidently

withstood the first world war as well as this one, for here the streets were narrow and cobbled with little alleys leading from one to the other, and the buildings were shabbily and comfortably grey, their façades broken here and there with wide curved archways closed by formidable wooden gates.

The Hôtel d'Angleterre straddled one of these arches. Its huge gates stood open, revealing a courtyard, a few wilted geraniums in pots, some crates of empty bottles and, at the end, tumbledown stables. A battered enamel plaque on the wall of the archway showed that in 1929 the Hôtel d'Angleterre had received recognition by an organisation calling itself Les Amis de la Route.

It's like old times, thought Hilary, remembering how often in the past he had thumbed the gastronomic guides before choosing his night's lodgings, then swung the car under just such an archway, proud of knowing the country well enough to eschew the big safe hotels and probe instead inside these small inns with their long tradition of friendly service and superlative meals. He walked up the steps in the left-hand wall of the deep arch and there, in a little alcove of an office sat madame, a bulbous hirsute old woman in the inevitable black dress, yellow-grey hair piled high on the top of her head, and surprisingly, very pale blue lascivious eyes popping too far from under their yellow wrinkled lids.

'Good day,' said Hilary, setting his bag on the floor and leaning over the counter. 'Have you by any chance a room for the night?'

'Single or double?' snapped madame, without interest.

Then she looked up and said, her pale eyes sharp with curiosity, 'But surely monsieur is English?'

'Yes,' admitted Hilary, unconsciously expecting now some warmth to the liberator, the prodigal son. Madame said without even making a pretence of looking in the big book that lay open before her, 'Monsieur is in A—— on business?'

'Yes,' agreed Hilary again.

'Monsieur is perhaps a commercial traveller?' madame enquired.

'No, I'm not,' said Hilary. He asked angrily, 'Have you or haven't you got a room?'

Madame said coldly, 'Monsieur must pardon my curiosity. In these past years we have acquired the habit of being suspicious of strangers.' Now she looked at her book and Hilary looked too, seeing plainly that hardly any names were filled in against the numbers down the page. 'Mariette' called madame angrily, and then, as a little shrivelled old servant nervously appeared, 'Mariette, show monsieur the number 24.'

The maid picked a key off the board and stood waiting at the foot of the stairs. But Hilary, remembering advice he had been given, still lingered. 'May I ask, madame,' he said politely, 'what will be the price of the room?'

Madame said coolly, 'We can discuss that when monsieur discovers whether he wishes to take it or not,' and started scratching violent entries on to a page of her ledger.

The old trout has got it in for me good and proper, thought Hilary, following the maid's black felt slippers up the narrow stone staircase, down a narrow corridor, round

corners and up and down unexpected little stairs. I'll have to produce some sort of reason for being here, he thought and then the maid threw open the door of number 24, padded across the room to open the shutters, and stood mutely waiting for Hilary's comments.

It was a room that he instantly recognised – the beige distempered walls topped with a mock-Egyptian stencil, the wide beige wooden bed with the white stuff counterpane, the gimcrack wardrobe, the single light in its pink glass shade in the centre of the ceiling. And because he remembered much happiness in such rooms, he felt kindly to this one and said, 'Yes, this will do very well. What's the price of it?' and the maid replied nervously, 'Monsieur will have to discuss the price with madame.'

That means I'm going to be done, thought Hilary, but he obediently went downstairs and again faced madame through the little window. 'I will take the room,' he said in a voice that he tried to make warm and friendly. 'What will the price be?'

But madame was not to be placated by charm. She said, 'That would depend on whether monsieur wishes to take the room only for a night or for longer.'

Hilary had never considered how long he was going to stay in A——. Pierre had been making all the arrangements, and since he had discarded Pierre, he had looked no further ahead than the next immediate need. Now he found himself stammering, 'I really don't know,' and then, quickly, 'Suppose you tell me the price for a single night, and also the pension price in case I find I have to spend a few days here?'

Madame considered a moment, her eyes fixed calculatingly on his face. At last she said, 'Well, suppose we say –' and she named two prices, watching to see how he took them.

Hilary, doing rapid sums in his head, thought her suggestions fantastically exorbitant. But it could not be for long, and anyway he wasn't going to argue with this horrible woman. He said as curtly as he could, 'Very well. I will let you know later how long I shall be staying,' and then strode up to his room again.

* * *

'And now,' he thought, 'what do I do next?'

* * *

If only, he said to himself, I'd let Pierre come too. He saw Pierre now, not as the falsely recognised friend, but as the useful courier who would organise the expeditions, take the decisions, protect him from the old harridan in the glass-box downstairs. I am too intolerant, he told himself. Pierre's politics are his own business. I should have taken the help he was offering me and let it go at that. But he knew that to have let it go at that would not have been possible. The deep instinctive sympathy between himself and Pierre could never have been turned into mutually useful acquaintance.

Of course, it may be perfectly simple, he told himself. It may be clear right away that this is the wrong child. (How can it be clear? he wondered for an instant.) Then he said, In that case it will all be easy. I just go straight back to Paris, tell Pierre it's a washout (for he said that if this were not my child, then my

child would never be found) and then I can go home again to my writing and my reading and all the other substitutes I have found for emotion.

Then he smiled, for without his desiring it, there had come into his mind a vision of himself and Pierre and the child held together by love, the ordeal surmounted, the catharsis complete. It would be wonderful beyond words, he told himself dreamily – and then he realised what he was thinking. It can never be like that, he said, there is nothing left in me to make it possible that it should be like that. The traitor emotions of love and tenderness and pity must stay dead in me. I could not endure them to live and then die again.

Slowly, wearily, he swung himself off the bed where he was lying and prepared to take up the search again.

CHAPTER SIX

He walked some distance from the hotel before he asked a passer-by the way to the Orphanage of Notre-Dame-de-la-Pitié. He did not know what reasons made him wish to keep his business so absolutely secret; from the moment that Pierre had come to his mother's house that Christmas Day, he had never told anyone of the possibility that he had a son in France and he knew that he never would tell anyone until the matter was concluded. And even then, unless the boy was found, claimed and rescued, no one should ever know other than that Hilary's son had died long long ago.

He walked, as he had been directed, to the outskirts of the town, in the opposite direction from the slag-heaps and the railway station. Here were the villas of prosperous retired tradesmen, each set in its little plot of ground with walls topped by high railings around it, all aping the nineteenth-century châteaux of the still more prosperous businessmen of the Second Empire.

The orphanage was one of these villas, larger but far shabbier than its neighbours down the street. A wide parterre of untended gravel led to the pretentious front door with the small double row of steps. There were no flowers in front of

the house; only a few dusty bushes straggled round the edge of the gravel, and at one side of the building Hilary could see an untidy cluster of huts stretching away behind it. With infinite apprehension he climbed the steps and rang the bell.

The door was opened by a small fat nun in a white habit, black crucifix hanging from her girdle, an enormous whiskered pimple sprouting from her red chin. Hilary said, 'Is it possible for me to see the Mother Superior? I am Monsieur Wainwright from England, I believe that she is expecting me –.' He was embarrassed by not knowing how to address her. He fumbled in his wallet, produced a card and handed it to the nun who peered at it gravely through round steel-rimmed spectacles, then opened a door, said, 'Will you wait in here, monsieur?' and went away.

He had been shown into a waiting-room, chilly and oppressive with its air of disuse and formality. Its walls were covered with a crimson damask paper, dating, surely, from the days when it was the dining-room of a solid bourgeois family, and it was still almost filled by a long mahogany table covered by a plush cloth and flanked by two rows of heavy mahogany chairs. The lower part of the long narrow window was covered with a paper imitating stained-glass in hexagons of ugly red and green. An ill-printed religious magazine lay on the table, but Hilary did not pick it up, only waited stiffly, tensely on one of the hard uncomfortable chairs. He waited for about ten minutes and then the door opened, and another nun in white came in.

This woman was tall and thin and in her face was the dispassionate competence of the good hospital nurse, or

rather, of the hospital sister, for it was apparent that she
held authority and a capacity for administration. Hilary felt
immediate respect for her as he politely rose to his feet and
responded to her cool interested greeting.

'Will you come into my office?' she said. 'We can talk more
easily there,' and he followed her into a little crowded room,
distinguished from other offices only by the crucifix hanging
on the wall over the desk.

Hilary found himself saying, 'Please will you tell me how
I should address you? I am not a Catholic, and so, you see, I
don't know –'

The Mother Superior smiled, and said, 'You should
call me "ma mère" and the sisters you should call "ma sœur".'
She paused a moment, looking thoughtfully at Hilary, and
then went on, 'Your friend, Monsieur Verdier, has explained
to me very clearly your position, and I can well understand
how much you hope that this child under our care may be
the one you seek. But there is one thing I must say at the
beginning. You are not, monsieur, a Catholic, as you have
just told me. Now, all the children here are Catholic. You
will understand that we must be very very certain that the
child is yours before we allow him to pass into a non-Catholic
home.'

Hilary said, almost casually, 'Oh, but my son would be a
Catholic. My wife was Catholic, you see, and it was promised
when we married that our children would be brought up in
that faith.' The point seemed unimportant to him. He had
passed through years of aggressive atheism, and now felt
greater sympathy with Catholicism than with the Church into

which he had been born, and for which his mother had exacted a meaningless respect.

'Ah!' said the Mother Superior and narrowed her eyes. 'That may make a certain difference.' She said in a brisker tone, 'Now what would you like me to tell you about little Jean?'

'Jean?' said Hilary eagerly. 'Why do you call him Jean? My boy's name was John. Did he tell you his name was Jean? They sound almost the same, don't they?' He was leaning across the table, trembling with excitement.

The nun said compassionately, 'I am afraid that the name is no more than a coincidence. When the child first came to us, he called himself Boubou which was, I understand, the name that the laundress had given him, and he was unable to give us any indication of his own name. So when we baptised him it was necessary to give him a name, and by chance we chose Jean.' She smiled sadly at him.

Hilary asked, 'And apart from his name? Did he say anything else about himself?'

'We questioned him very closely when he first came,' said the nun, 'in case we could find out anything that might help us one day to restore him to his family. But you must remember that the boy was very young – about two and a half, the doctor said. He was unable to tell us anything constructive about himself, and, of course, we could not know what to ask. It is possible that if you had been there, you could have asked the right questions –' she broke off, and added with a smile, 'but you are here now, and perhaps God will put it into your heart to ask the right questions even now. But you must remember

that three years have passed and that what a child remembers when he is two, he will have forgotten when he is five.'

'That is what we thought,' agreed Hilary. He suddenly wanted to ask if the nun saw any striking likeness between himself and this child, but he was afraid of the answer, positive or negative. Instead he said, 'Where is the boy – where is Jean now?'

'He is out for a walk,' replied the nun. 'The bigger boys are still doing their lessons, but the little ones stop work at half-past four and then Sister Clothilde takes them out walking for an hour. This will give us time, monsieur, to decide what to do.'

It was apparent that the Mother Superior had already in fact decided what should be done, and Hilary, comforted to let decision pass from him again, said, 'I shall be happy to do whatever you advise.'

'Since the war ended,' said the nun, 'some of our boys have left us. Our children are not all orphans, you understand. Sometimes they are the children of parents who are divorced, sometimes for one reason or another the home is altogether unsatisfactory, or perhaps there is only one parent who finds the burden too much. During the war years, many of our boys had fathers who were prisoners of war, and now these are returning home and often coming to collect their sons.'

She sighed. 'We are glad for the little ones who can go back to homes of their own,' she said, 'but when this happens it makes for great sadness for those who are left, and more, in many it raises hope that may not – often cannot be realised. And so I am sure, monsieur, that it is not right that little Jean

should know that you may be his father. With your permission, I shall tell him that you are a patron of Madame Quillebœuf and have come at her request to see that he is well and happy.'

'I entirely agree,' said Hilary, his burden diminishing under this cool competent control.

'It is a kindly lie,' said the Mother Superior with dignity, 'and we must all hope that we shall soon be able to explain to little Jean why we told it to him.' She waited for Hilary's assent to this statement and he managed to murmur, almost to groan agreement.

'But,' she said, 'our kindly lie has disadvantages as lies always must. I cannot think it right to disturb the routine of the boy too much in case, at the end, he must go back into it again. So this is what I suggest. If you can come here each evening at half-past five, when the day's work is over, I will allow the little Jean to go out with you until half-past seven, when the small ones go to bed. This is the regular arrangement when visitors come to see the children and there will seem nothing remarkable about it. After you have known the boy for a week or so, I feel sure that you will be able to know whether he is your son.'

'So you don't believe in instinct?' asked Hilary impulsively, remembering Pierre.

'Yes,' she said, 'I believe in instinct – but in instinct tempered by reason. You, monsieur, will have an instinctive reaction when you see the child; I do not know you enough to guess whether this will be instinctive recognition or rejection.' (Yet you do know, thought Hilary, though I don't know

myself.) 'But the child's future is at stake, and yours too, monsieur. Such a matter cannot be decided without the most careful consideration.'

'You are right,' said Hilary, believing this, but inwardly he was appalled. He had so gladly accepted Pierre's theory of instantaneous recognition, the ordeal surmounted as soon as endured. A week – , he thought, and then refused to consider it.

'And now,' said the Mother Superior, standing up, 'perhaps you would like me to show you round our orphanage.'

'I should be delighted,' said Hilary, rising and following her. 'This is our little chapel,' she said, opening a door, and Hilary found himself in a small room – once, perhaps, the morning-room – with some hard chairs, an altar, a crude plaster statue of the Virgin, some poor religious pictures. The nun crossed herself and genuflected, and Hilary stood uneasily in the room, waiting till she should lead him out of it again.

'We are very proud of our chapel,' she said outside. 'We lost our little statue of the Virgin during the big raid – the vibration made it fall and shattered it – but thanks to the kindness of Madame Mercatel, who made a collection among the pious women of this town, we have been able to replace it. Madame Mercatel is the mother of our schoolmaster, whom you will meet.'

'Is yours a wealthy foundation, ma mère?' asked Hilary, following her up a broad polished staircase.

'Alas no,' said the nun, sighing, 'we are very poor indeed, and since the war we have been poorer than ever, just when

the need is greatest. But God will provide.' She bent her head reverently, and then opened a door, saying, 'This, monsieur, is one of the bedrooms.'

It was the poorest, saddest room Hilary had ever seen. There were some forty iron beds arranged in four tidy rows, two rows with their heads to the wall, two rows in the centre of the room. Each bed was covered with a thin grey blanket. By each bed stood a wooden chair. There was no other furniture. There was no covering on the wooden floor, no pictures on the dark green distempered walls. There were no toys. Each bed was anonymous and identical.

'This is the youngest children's room,' said the nun. 'It is here that your – that the little Jean sleeps. This, I think, is his bed.' She walked to a bed in the middle of the room and then looked down at it, and shook her head, saying sadly, 'Oh, naughty Jean.'

'Why, what has he done?' asked Hilary, following her.

In the middle of the grey blanket someone had placed a little pile of things. There was a pinecone, a stone marble with nearly all its colour rubbed away, a used American stamp, and a tiny little celluloid swan with its head broken off and a dirty piece of rag tied round its neck for a bandage.

'What's it all about?' Hilary asked.

The Mother Superior laughed. 'The children *will* hide things in their beds,' she explained. 'They know it means the loss of a mark if they are found out, but we can't stop them doing it. I'm afraid that your –' this time she did not correct the pronoun, '– your little Jean is a very bad offender.'

Hilary asked, 'What does the loss of a mark entail?'

'Most of our children have families or relations who take them for the school holidays,' the nun replied. 'For such, every ten marks lost means a day off their holidays. For little Jean, it will not, in fact, mean very much, except, of course, that it is felt as a great disgrace to lose marks. Some of our boys are too big for women to beat, monsieur, and we have to use such methods to maintain discipline.'

She turned away from the bed and passed on through the dormitory, through other dormitories, through the washrooms and the laundry, each room reeking with the peculiar, the unmistakable smell of institutional poverty, and Hilary followed her and made appropriate comments, while all the while he found that he was silently repeating:

A box of counters and a red-vein'd stone,
A piece of glass abraded by the beach,
And six or seven shells,
A bottle with bluebells,
And two French copper coins, ranged there with
*   careful art,*
To comfort his sad heart . . .

But this child had not even such a choice of treasures to comfort *him*, Hilary thought suddenly, remembering the pitiful heap on the bed. They came down the stairs into the hall again and the nun said, 'We have still some time before the children come back. Would you like to see the schoolrooms?'

'Very much,' said Hilary, welcoming what must surely be

a respite from the intolerable pity that was obsessing him. He asked, 'Do the children get all their lessons here?'

'All,' said the nun. 'We keep them here till they are fourteen, and then they take an examination. Those who do well pass into our establishment at Marly where they have four years' training as apprentices and leave with a good trade at their fingertips. The others, alas, must find work right away.'

Now she led him outside the house and into a large wooden hut. A corridor ran its full length and behind the flimsy wall Hilary could hear children's voices raised in the familiar rhythms of repetition.

'I must take you into each one,' said the nun, 'it would never do to leave one out, but it is Monsieur Mercatel whom I am anxious you should meet.' She turned the door handle and they went into the first room.

Some thirty boys instantly sprang to their feet and stood facing the visitors, their arms folded high across their chests. They were dressed in a varied range of poor clothing, their ages running from about ten to twelve. The nun led Hilary before them to where a young frizzy-haired woman in a jumper and skirt stood waiting by her desk.

'This is Monsieur Wainwright, a visitor from England,' said the Mother Superior, 'and this, monsieur, is Mademoiselle Lucille who comes to instruct our boys in geography and history.'

Hilary shook hands with the young woman who looked away from him, seeming painfully shy. The Mother Superior said graciously. 'It is geography now, is it not? I wonder if any of you can tell Monsieur Wainwright the capital of England?

Yes, perhaps Louis?' she pointed at a little curly-haired negro who said, 'London!' with an enormous proud grin. The nun, the teacher and the children all looked expectantly at Hilary.

This was the sort of audience to which he could respond with ease. He said with enthusiasm, 'That's really very good, Louis. I'm sure that I didn't know the capital of France when I was as old as you,' and the boys all smiled at him sycophantically, obviously longing for the respite from lessons to continue.

But the conventions had been satisfied. The Mother Superior said, 'Now we must not interrupt the class any longer,' waited while Hilary bowed a polite farewell to Mademoiselle Lucille, and then led the way from the room.

'I thought the sisters would do the teaching,' said Hilary in some surprise.

'No,' said the nun, 'we are not a teaching order. The care of the boys is our task, but their instructors all come daily from the town. Now here,' she said, 'the second class are taking their reading lesson under Madame Lapointe.'

Madame Lapointe was instantly recognisable as a competent professional teacher. The walls of her classroom were decorated with pinned-up pictures, children's drawings in crayon, illustrations from teachers' magazines. She was plump and middle-aged, and she and the Mother Superior greeted each other with the cool respect of efficient colleagues. The same formula was observed. Red-haired Robert read aloud the fable of the fox and the piece of cheese and Hilary wished, to the boys' delight, that he could speak French with so pure an accent, and then withdrew to the corridor again.

'And now,' said the nun, 'we come to the biggest boys who are learning mathematics with Monsieur Mercatel. I must tell you that he is the only one of my colleagues who knows the true reason for your visit to us. He is, I know, anxious to have an opportunity to discuss the boy with you.'

Some of Hilary's natural elation at being the honoured guest on the familiar platform withered as he followed the Mother Superior into the last room of the hut.

Again the boys sprang to their feet and crossed their arms over their chests, big boys this time, and seeming, Hilary thought fleetingly, more rugged, more developed than English boys of the same age. But his interest was for the teacher who was coming to greet the visitors, his hand outstretched in welcome.

He looks like an Englishman, was Hilary's first thought, but he did not. He might have been a native of any country, this small thin grey-haired gentleman, kindly mouth, mild blue eyes, the cultured European of true goodness and no importance whatsoever.

'You are studying geometry to-day, are you not?' said the Mother Superior when the introduction had been performed. 'I do not know if that is a subject that interests you, Monsieur Wainwright?'

'Poets are seldom interested in geometry,' commented Monsieur Mercatel with a smile at Hilary, who felt disproportionately pleased that this man should know of him in his own right, not merely as the father seeking his lost son.

'Even for the edification of your boys I cannot pretend to be interested in geometry,' he said aloud, smiling with

friendliness at the class. 'But perhaps among them you also have some poets who feel about it as I do?'

Everyone laughed and Monsieur Mercatel said, 'Georges is better than he should be at writing poems that have nothing to do with his lessons,' and a tall boy in the front row giggled in shamefaced confusion. 'But I do not think,' continued Monsieur Mercatel, 'that his poems will ever have the reputation of yours.'

Now the needs of the boys had been satisfied and they could be left, still standing with their arms folded, while the three adults stood by the diagrams on the blackboard and talked in low voices.

'I was wondering,' said Monsieur Mercatel, 'whether it would be possible for you, monsieur, to come to a café with me one evening so that we could make one another's better acquaintance?'

'I should be delighted,' said Hilary, meaning it, thinking only that this would be a pleasant meeting, not at all of the talk about the boy.

'Tomorrow?' suggested Monsieur Mercatel, and Hilary agreeing, he went on, 'So shall I fetch you at your hotel at eight o'clock? Where are you staying?'

'At the Hôtel d'Angleterre,' said Hilary, and saw with surprise the distaste on both their faces. Monsieur Mercatel said with a shrug, 'One forgets there is no longer anywhere else,' and then good-byes were said and Hilary and the Mother Superior left the room.

'Ma mère,' said Hilary timidly as they walked back along the corridor, 'What is wrong with the Hôtel d'Angleterre?'

The nun hesitated a moment as if wondering whether to answer. Then she said reluctantly, 'As a Christian one should be charitable, monsieur, but as a Frenchwoman it is difficult to refrain from making judgments. We all can see that the position of an hotel-keeper is difficult under an Occupation, but there were some who brought out their worst wines for the Germans and some who brought out their best. Monsieur Leblanc was one of the latter.'

'How unpleasant,' said Hilary. 'Do you mean he was a collaborationist?'

'Oh, no,' said the nun. 'The Leblancs would never have enough courage to take bold action, not even wrong action. There were, of course, some people who thought they should have been tried when the war was over, but there would have been no point in trying such. It was most unfortunate that the other hotels were bombed. The townspeople kept away from the Hôtel d'Angleterre for a time, but people forget very quickly – and perhaps one should not wish that they should bear rancour too long.'

'They didn't seem at all pleased to see me at the hotel,' said Hilary thoughtfully. They were walking now across an open gravel yard.

'They are cowardly people,' said the nun contemptuously. 'They probably thought that, being an Englishman, you had come to bring retribution.' She dismissed the subject and said in her former manner, 'And this, monsieur, is where the children play.'

'I see,' said Hilary. There was no comment he could make on the bare empty yard and they crossed it silently and re-entered the house.

A bell began to clang.

'Ah,' said the nun, 'now lessons are over to-day, and the small boys should be back from their walk. If you will wait a little, monsieur, I will send Jean to you as soon as he has had something to eat, and then, if you wish, you may take him out with you.'

She shut Hilary into the waiting-room again, and went away, and he sat there frozen in thought and feeling, looking at the geometrical paper on the window, imagining the hexagons into this pattern and that, all ugly, all pointless, all wholly unsatisfactory. Time stopped for him while he sat there waiting.

Then he heard the door handle turning, slipping back and turning again under the fumbling hands. He stood up and faced the door. The little boy came in and in the instant before his eyes perceived the child there was torn from his blood, his body, his very consciousness the conviction that this was his son.

PART THREE
The Ordeal

CHAPTER SEVEN

Monday

And then he looked at the child.

And told himself with a kind of horror, 'How could I ever have imagined that this child was mine!'

* * *

For insensibly a picture of his son had been forming in his mind. He did not know this; if he tried consciously to imagine a boy who might be his, his conscious mind gave no response. But his unconscious mind retained as the image of his son the child in the snapshot that he had refused to send to Pierre, the five-year-old English boy in his grey flannel shorts and blazer, short grey socks, neat brown walking shoes, wide laughing eyes under the grey felt hat, and a cheerful confident grin. In his memory of this picture his deepest expectations of recognition were founded.

But facing him was a thin little boy in a black sateen overall. Its sleeves were too short and from them dangled red swollen hands too big for the frail wrists. Hilary looked from these painful hands to the little boy's long thin grubby legs,

to the crude coarse socks falling over shabby black boots that were surely several sizes too large. It's a foreign child, he thought numbly, and then he let himself look at the small white face turned towards him, a lock of black hair falling from a travesty of a parting over enormous dark eyes that stared imploringly into his.

He knew that he should have moved towards the child, greeted him naturally and with friendliness. But he could only stand and stare with horror and repulsion, saying wildly to himself, 'Why does he look at me like that? He doesn't know why I'm here. Why does he look at me like that?'

He suddenly remembered as he stood there, trying desperately to move forward to the casual greeting, his Aunt Jessie telling him that in his early childhood, whenever she used to visit him at his home, he would stand by her chair in the drawing-room with huge imploring eyes fixed upon her and she would know that he was saying 'Please take me back to the farm with you; please take me back to the farm.' 'But he doesn't know who I am,' he repeated to himself, and then the door opened behind the child and the Mother Superior came in, a child's coat over her arm.

Her eyes flickered from one to the other, and she said briskly, 'Well, have you introduced yourselves yet? Jean, this is the English gentleman I was telling you about, Monsieur Wainwright. Go and shake hands with him at once. I don't know where your manners are.'

The child came slowly forward, his eyes still fixed on Hilary's face. He put out his hand, and as Hilary touched its iciness, the intensity that had held them both was broken. The

boy dropped his eyes to the ground and Hilary breathed deeply and felt half-dead with weariness.

The Mother Superior seemed to notice nothing. She went on in the same cheerful voice, 'Monsieur is going to spend a few days here and then he's going back to Paris to tell Madame Quillebœuf all about you.' She added with a note of anxiety, 'Jean, you remember Madame Quillebœuf, don't you?'

The boy looked apprehensive. Hilary thought, He's become scared of questions, and an impulse to spare the child made him say quickly, with assurance not interrogation in his voice, 'But of course you remember Grandmaman.'

Miraculously the boy's expression changed. Now he looked at Hilary again, but this time his eyes were full of relief and gratitude as if he had already received what he was asking for. He said, 'She had a clock. A bird jumped out and said, "Cuckoo".' The words were tumbling over each other with excitement.

Hilary thought, How queer to hear him talking French, and simultaneously, That must be the clock that the old lady sold. The nun was saying, 'I too had a clock like that when I was a little girl in Alsace,' and the boy quickly turned to her the face of another child, a child vivid, eager, interested.

Now the Mother Superior was saying smoothly, 'I mustn't keep you both indoors talking, when I am sure you want to set out on your walk. Come here, Jean,' she said, and helped him into the heavy straight black coat, buttoned it tightly, and pulled the hood up over his head. Then she opened the door and stood quietly waiting beside it until Hilary and Jean had

passed her, and then she closed the door behind them and left them together in the hall.

Hilary turned the handle of the front door, but the door wouldn't open. The boy darted forward and said eagerly, 'Let me. I know how to.' He stood on tiptoe to release a high latch, then pulled the door open and proudly held it back for Hilary to pass through.

* * *

It had grown cold while Hilary had been inside the orphanage, cold and dark. The colours were fading from the trees and the walls, and a thin damp mist was rising from the ground. What the devil shall we do, he thought in dismay, and he turned to the child waiting beside him and said, 'You'll have to tell me where to go, because I don't know your town at all.'

Jean said breathlessly, 'Do you like trains, monsieur?'

'I like trains very much,' said Hilary, hopefully.

'There is a level-crossing,' said Jean, 'I think – do you think monsieur – it would be nice to go that way?'

'Nothing could be nicer,' said Hilary. 'Come on, you show me where it is,' and they walked down the steps together.

Outside the gate Jean stopped and looked up at Hilary doubtfully. 'Yes,' said Hilary, as he might have reassured a dog. 'I do really want to see the trains,' and suddenly the boy seemed sure of him and for the first time gave him a natural happy little boy's grin. 'Robert said it was this way,' he said, and they started off down the hill.

At first Jean walked sedately by Hilary's side, every now and then glancing sideways up into his face. Each time he did

so, Hilary found he must inevitably smile at him, telling him without words that all was and would be well, and at last the boy seemed reassured. He started to run about, a few steps this way, a few steps that, sometimes running just a little ahead, but always quickly coming back to look into Hilary's face and, at last, to smile at Hilary before Hilary smiled at him.

'Look!' said Hilary after they had gone a hundred yards or so, 'There's your level-crossing right at the bottom of the hill,' and he pointed down a side turning to the tall posts reared erect beside the road.

Jean stood still and put his head on one side and looked at them. Then, one last glance at Hilary, and he started to run down the hill.

Hilary lengthened his stride to keep close behind. He didn't have to lengthen it very much. The thin legs in the clumsy boots were incapable of going very fast and Hilary and Jean reached the bottom of the hill together.

Just as they arrived, the heavy posts fell slowly and majestically over the road, their dangling iron curtains hitting the ground with a splendid clang. Jean clutched Hilary's coat and said with a kind of ecstatic tremor, 'Robert said that after the gates go down the train comes,' and at that moment they both heard the chuff of the engine coming towards them.

It was a slow old goods-engine dragging what seemed to Hilary a really surprising number of coal-filled wagons and it took a long time to pass. He watched it with the absorption a passing train can always command and momentarily forgot the little boy at his side. Then the last wagon went by and the

rumble and clatter slowly died away and Hilary heard a small incredulous voice saying, 'I've seen a train.'

Hilary demanded, 'Haven't you ever seen a train before?'

The boy was frightened at Hilary's tone. He said, 'No, monsieur,' and his eyes opened widely in apprehension.

'But don't you ever come this way on your walks?' asked Hilary.

'No, monsieur,' whispered Jean, 'we always go the other way.' His eyes pleaded for forgiveness.

It's unbelievable, thought Hilary savagely, it's intolerable and I can't stand it. Then he looked at Jean and saw that he, completely uncomprehending, was finding this moment intolerable too, and with an effort of deliberate physical relaxation he made himself say warmly, 'Look, Jean, the gates are still down. I think another train's going to come.'

They waited and watched a rusty tank engine puff strenuously by. 'Look, monsieur,' shouted Jean, 'Look, it's going backwards' and he burst into wild laughter, and Hilary laughed with him.

Then the gates went up again and Hilary discovered that he was feeling cold. He suggested, 'Let's go to that café over the road and sit in the warm. We can still see the trains out of the window.'

Jean nodded quickly, grinning to show how much he liked the idea, and followed Hilary into the café.

Inside it was warm and comfortable. A big stove was burning in one corner and rexine-covered benches backed with high boards made convenient private alcoves. Hilary set the child near the window at an empty table and sat down facing him.

'Now,' he said, 'what would you like to drink?'

Jean looked puzzled, and Hilary realising that a café was as novel an experience as a train ordered a beer and a raspberry syrup.

'It's a pretty colour,' Jean said timorously when this was set before him. 'Taste it,' urged Hilary, and Jean tasted and then drank the whole lot down with loud sucking gulps. 'Well, what do you think of it?' Hilary asked, and Jean said boldly, 'I even think I could drink another,' and Hilary laughed and ordered it for him.

Jean seemed to have forgotten about the trains. His eyes were roving the room now with eager interest. 'Look, monsieur,' he cried suddenly, pointing to a dusty green plant in a pot, 'Look, there's a little palm tree.'

'How do you know it's a palm tree?' asked Hilary, interested.

'I saw it in a book,' Jean said casually.

'Do you like reading?' Hilary pursued.

Jean said, 'I like reading about Africa.'

'And what else?' asked Hilary.

Jean said, 'I haven't got a book about anything else.'

Hilary frowned. He resented his own inability to anticipate the to him unbelievable limitations of this child's experience. Then again he remembered that he had a part to play in which a frown was a forbidden indulgence and asked quickly, 'What do you learn about Africa?'

'I know about black mambas,' said Jean. 'They curl up in trees and hide and when you go by they spit in your eye and what they spit is poison and then you have to die, no one can save you.'

'In London where I come from,' said Hilary, 'there's a place called a Zoo where every kind of wild animal lives –,' The boy interrupted to demand avidly, 'Do they eat people?' and Hilary answered, 'No, they don't eat people because they're all shut up in different cages so that they can't hurt anyone. Well, when I was a little boy, my' – he was going to say 'my father' – but he changed it to, 'I used to be taken to the Zoo and one day I was taken to the house where the snakes are and the man who looks after them took an enormous python out of its cage and hung it right round my neck.' The boy gave a delighted sigh and gazed joyfully at Hilary while he talked about the panda and the giraffes and the elephants – 'You can go for rides on the elephant's back,' he said and found that he wanted to add, 'I'll take you on an elephant one day.'

But he did not. He looked at the small white face turned so absorbedly to his and asked abruptly, 'What did you have to eat before you came out with me?'

'Some bread and a lump of sugar,' answered Jean. 'We always have that after lessons.' His eyes searched Hilary's face, looking for approbation.

'And for lunch?' said Hilary. 'What did you have for lunch?'

The boy dropped his eyes and said, 'I don't remember.'

Help me to be slow and careful, prayed Hilary, he didn't know to whom. He said in a deliberately cheerful voice, 'Now when I was a little boy, the thing I liked best to eat was fried potatoes. Whenever I could choose what I wanted for lunch, that was what I chose.'

He was succeeding, Jean was watching him again, the dull defensive look fading from his eyes. He said cautiously, 'I think I'd like fried potatoes, too.'

But now Hilary was stuck again. He could think of no food that it was probable the little boy had ever tasted. He tried, 'Will you tell me about the book you read – the book about Africa?'

It seemed that this was a different sort of question, a question not to be shied from but embraced. Jean said, 'It belongs to Madame Lapointe. I read it during reading-lessons, because I can read and the other boys in my class can't. And madame gives me the book and I sit at the back and read it all the time.'

'But how is it,' Hilary asked, 'that you can read and the other boys can't?'

Jean answered simply, 'I don't know, monsieur,' but this time he was not evading the question; he was offering Hilary the truth.

The wireless that had been ceaselessly droning dance music now abruptly switched to speech, and Hilary noticing it for the first time, glanced at his watch. 'It's a quarter-past seven,' he said, trying as hard as he could to keep relief from his voice. 'We'll have to be getting back or the Mother Superior will be angry with me.'

He rose, and silently the little boy slid from the seat and stood waiting, and again in his eyes was the agonised entreaty with which he had first greeted his visitor. Hilary found himself saying very gently, 'It's all right, Jean, it's all right. I'm coming to take you out again tomorrow and the next day too.'

Without changing his expression the little boy asked, 'And the day after that?'

'Well, I don't know about that,' said Hilary, uneasily. 'We'll have to see about that, won't we?' and the child looked quickly at the ground and Hilary could no longer see the big imploring eyes. 'Come on,' he said, and he walked quickly out of the café, the boy following behind him.

They started to walk up the hill in silence, Jean keeping close to Hilary's side. It was dark now, and the lights from a few unshuttered windows were all they had to see by. Gradually the boy began to lag behind and Hilary, at last noticing this, said with the tenderness of compunction, 'Jean, are you tired?'

A small voice said with a quaver, 'No, monsieur.'

'But I am,' said Hilary. 'Won't you take my hand so that we can help each other up the hill?' He put out his own hand and firmly grasped the child's which was icily, inhumanly cold. He said with agony, 'Haven't you got any gloves?'

'No, monsieur,' said Jean sadly. You could hear in his voice how much he regretted the answer he knew must displease. Then he offered hopefully, 'Robert has gloves, he has blue ones. His aunt made them for him.'

Hilary remembered, 'Isn't Robert the one with red hair?'

'Yes,' said Jean.

'He ought to have red gloves to match his red hair,' said Hilary, and the joke delighted the child, made him laugh gleefully and quickened his step a little up the hill.

They turned in at the gate and Hilary started towards the front door to feel Jean tugging at his hand. 'What is it?' he

asked, and Jean said anxiously, 'We're not allowed to go in that way, monsieur. There's a door at the side.'

'It's all right if you're with me,' Hilary said reassuringly. He remembered the first time his father came to see him at prep school, his dread lest any convention should be transgressed. Then he wondered if Jean's fear was only a conventional one like his own, and explained, 'You see, I must give you back properly or perhaps they won't lend you to me again,' and they climbed the steps and Hilary rang the bell.

The door was opened again by the fat bewhiskered nun and Hilary, watching closely, saw that she and Jean spontaneously and lovingly smiled at each other before she said, 'Now you say "thank you" nicely to monsieur, and then run off to bed – quick.'

'Thank you, monsieur,' Jean said colourlessly and obediently, and then he remembered something – perhaps the trains, perhaps the raspberry syrup, perhaps the elephants at the Zoo – and lifted glowing eyes to Hilary and said fervently, 'Oh, thank you, monsieur,' and then turned and ran away, his boots clip-clopping on the checkered marble floor as he went.

'He's a nice child,' said the nun, half-roughly, half-lovingly, and then, 'The Mother Superior asks, monsieur, if you will take a cup of coffee with her before you go?' and Hilary, longing to be alone, longing to examine his thoughts and emotions in privacy, longing to escape, could only bow politely and say that he would be delighted.

CHAPTER EIGHT

Monday – continued

The Mother Superior was in her little crowded office, writing under a dim bare bulb. When Hilary came in she laid down her pen and lifted her tired eyes, saying with politeness that was clearly none the less genuine for having no warmth in it, 'I thought you might like some coffee before you start back to your hotel. It is such a cold night.'

'It's very good of you,' Hilary said, sitting down.

'Not at all,' said the nun. After a moment she added, 'It is seldom that I am able to finish my work early enough to give myself the pleasure of receiving visitors,' and Hilary knew that she was reassuring him, telling him that after to-night's ceremonial visit he would be free to bring back the child and quietly depart.

The same fat nun came in with two large cups of coffee on a tray and set it down on the desk. 'Thank you, Sister Thérèse,' said the Mother Superior. 'Has little Jean gone up to bed now?'

'Yes, ma mère,' said the old nun, 'and so tired that I hardly knew what to do with him.' In her voice was the oblique grudging reproach of the solicitous nanny.

'It's only from pleasure,' said the Mother Superior placatingly. 'You'll find he'll sleep it off, ma sœur,' and Sister Thérèse muttered pessimistically, 'Let us hope so,' and withdrew.

The Mother Superior laughed gently, and then handed Hilary his coffee. 'It's not real coffee, I'm afraid,' she apologised. 'Real coffee is virtually unobtainable now.'

'I wish I'd known,' said Hilary with contrition, ashamed that he had not thought to bring such a simple welcome gift, and then he tasted the brew in his cup. Its nastiness so surprised him that he was quite unable to prevent his face twisting into an expression of unsuppressible disgust. He tried to apologise quickly, but the Mother Superior would have none of it. She said laughingly, 'We are always told that the English make bad coffee, but I can see from your face that it is not as bad as this.'

'No, indeed,' said Hilary vehemently. 'Madame –' he remembered and corrected himself, 'ma mère, is this really all that is available in France?'

'Except on the Black Market,' said the nun. 'It is hard, is it not? The two things we French care most about are good bread and good coffee and we can have neither.'

This talk of food reminded Hilary of the little boy. Forgetting how much he had dreaded the Mother Superior raising the subject, he asked, 'Do your children – do you get enough for your children to eat?'

'No,' said the Mother Superior, vehemently. 'We do not. The authorities do the best they can for us, but in these days our unhappy country has little food to offer to those who must buy in the cheapest market.'

'But aren't there any special arrangements for children?'

'Ah,' said the Mother Superior, 'I have heard of the admirable feeding of children in England, but we, monsieur, are not a disciplined people. We say that there must be eggs for children, but when you look for them in the market they are never to be found. We get a little milk, but only for children under six years. Meat we can hardly ever buy. We must all hope that soon conditions will get better, but in the meantime,' she spoke with passion, 'these are the most important years in our children's lives.'

'Is Jean healthy?' Hilary demanded.

She spoke carefully now. 'Yes, by our present standards he is healthy – but only by those standards. The doctor tells me he has a tendency to rickets; this will doubtless get worse, because soon he will be about six and then there will be no more milk for him – but then most of our children have a tendency to rickets. He is certainly anaemic. If he gets a cold, if he cuts his leg, it will take him longer than it should to recover, but that also is true of all our children. By the charts in my books that were written before the war, he does not weigh so much as he should, but that is to be expected; it is true that on this diet some children grow fat instead of staying too thin, as Jean does, but such is not a healthy fat. Also – and this is much to-day – Jean has not yet got tuberculosis.'

'Do you mean,' said Hilary, incredulously, 'that you have tubercular children here – among the healthy ones?'

'Yes,' said the nun steadily. 'We have tubercular children here. If you knew more of Europe, monsieur, you would know that to run the risk of being infected with tuberculosis in a

home where you have a bed to sleep in and regular meals is to-day to have a fortunate childhood.'

Hilary was unable to believe what she was saying. He argued, 'But surely there are special homes for the tubercular?'

The nun said, 'Those are full.' Her lips were tightly closed as if she wished to say more but would not, then she released them to cry passionately, 'Monsieur, you English do not begin to comprehend what Europe is like to-day. You find that conditions in France are bad – believe me, monsieur, we are in Paradise. You could not begin to believe what I have been told by our sisters who have been working in Germany, in Austria, in Poland. When I could weep for our own children, then I remember what I have been told of those others.' She stopped sharply.

Hilary said sincerely from his heart, 'Ma mère, you must forgive me. I have become unused to pity, these past years – and to-day it has overwhelmed me.'

'No, monsieur,' said the nun. 'It is you who must forgive me. But I must not keep you any more from your dinner. Tomorrow, when you come, I will have Jean ready and waiting for you.' She stood up and Hilary rose too, and said good-bye.

At the door he turned, remembering what he wished to ask, 'Excuse me ma mère, but who provides the clothes for your children?'

'It is our rule,' she answered, 'that the families and patrons of our children must keep them clothed. Sometimes, of course, this is not possible, and then, with charitable help, we provide.'

'Would there be any objection,' Hilary asked hesitatingly, his hand on the door, 'if I bought Jean a pair of gloves?'

'None at all,' said the nun, and her smile was warm, human, unconventual.

* * *

Hilary was famished; he had had neither lunch nor tea to-day, and back at the hotel he made his way straight into the dining-room, and sat down at a table in the corner.

If ever a remembrance of good eating had pervaded this room, it had now been utterly dissipated. Few of the tables had even been laid, and on those that were, no clean white papers covered the stains on the torn cloths. Two men who looked like commercial travellers were eating together at a table nearby; for the rest, the room was deserted. Cracks ran across the plaster on the ceiling, huge stains blotched the walls, and the long serving table that should have been covered with baskets of fruit, with dishes of ham, with lobster and cold fish intricately garnished, held only a few pepper-pots, some bottles of sauce, some empty tarnished vases. It was incredible, thought Hilary, that any French dining-room should wear an air as forbidding and desolate as an English provincial café, but this one had succeeded in doing so.

The maid scuttled towards him with a menu card. He could have, he found, some soup, some rissoles, some fruit. There was nothing else listed at all.

He asked in dismay, 'Haven't you got anything better than this?'

The maid said nervously, 'I will ask,' and scuttled away again. She came back to whisper, 'Monsieur says if you wish, you can have some pâté to begin with, and after that, an entrecôte grillée, some haricots, some pommes frites?'

'Then I will certainly have all that,' said Hilary decidedly. The maid prepared to go, came back again to add timorously, 'Madame said that you will understand that this is *en supplément*?'

'That's all right,' said Hilary, not understanding or bothering to try. He ordered a bottle of vin ordinaire, and prepared, once more, to enjoy a meal in France.

But he could not. Last night's superb meal he had accepted with wonderment, with delight, but without any hint of guilt. Now, tasting his crisp splendidly greasy potatoes, he found himself remembering the little boy who wasn't quite sure what these were. Cutting his juicy steak he heard the Mother Superior saying, 'Meat we can hardly ever buy.' He looked across to the men at the centre table. They too were eating large hunks of meat and seemingly quite untroubled by remorse. This is Black Market, Hilary told himself, it's what we've all been so shocked about, what prevents the poor getting even enough, and then he asked, But what good does it do if I refuse it? It won't go to those children, it will only go to other people rich enough to pay for it, and he ate it, and argued with himself, knowing that he should go hungry and that he would not.

'I'll have some coffee,' he said at the end and the maid whispered, 'Real coffee, monsieur?' He nodded, unwilling to give his assent in words and the real coffee arrived, black

and fragrant, real French coffee, and as he drank it he remembered the orphanage brew.

A man in a dirty chef's uniform was standing beside the table. His grey hair was cut short to form a matted thatch all over his head, his blue eyes were small and too closely set together, his hands perpetually washing each other. He said obsequiously, 'Monsieur has enjoyed his meal?'

'Yes, thank you,' said Hilary with distaste, hoping the creature would go. But he still waited, and Hilary forced himself to ask politely, 'You are the *patron*?'

'I am,' said the man. He bent over Hilary's chair, and added in a carefully lowered tone, 'Anything monsieur wants, he has only to ask for. That menu, you understand – it is only for show.'

'Thank you,' said Hilary frigidly. The man's nearness was distasteful to him, but still he stood there, imparting confidences in his low conspiratorial voice.

'It is like old times to see an Englishman again,' he assured Hilary. 'Before the war, we had many English visitors. Often they would come back, year after year.'

He was clearly lying, thought Hilary. The town was not on the main routes from the coast to anywhere of significance. The *patron* bent lower and suggested, 'Monsieur is here on leave, eh?' Apparently he had been primed by madame as to the various reasons why monsieur was *not* here.

'No, I am not,' said Hilary. He forced himself to make an explanation. 'As a matter of fact I have come to visit the child of an old comrade of mine in the orphanage.'

'Ah,' said Monsieur Leblanc with a too sharp sigh of relief. Crocodile tears in his voice, he said, 'How it breaks one's heart

to think of the poor little children up there, orphaned by this terrible war.'

'Yes,' said Hilary meaningly, 'but at least they have the satisfaction of knowing that their fathers died as heroes.' He rose from his chair, Monsieur Leblanc leaping to pull it from under him and murmuring as he strode away, 'Remember, monsieur, anything we can do – you have only to ask.'

* * *

And now, said Hilary to himself, I will go for a little walk. Then I will go to a café, and have a cognac. Then, when I have cleared my head and cleansed my mind of the slime of this worm, I will think about to-day.

The moon had risen and was shining over the grey houses. Hilary walked without purpose, down this street, up that one, noticing little of what he saw, trying only to pass time until he could assure himself that the first item on his programme had been completed and he could proceed to the second. I'll wait till the next café, he told himself, and then on past the next one and the next, till at last he seated himself at a rusty iron table on the pavement.

He ordered himself a cognac and took out a cigarette. It was only a shabby little café, and there was no animation in any of the groups sitting near him under the weak dangling lamps. Two girls sauntered by in short pleated tartan skirts and long white knitted jackets, stopped to glance curiously at Hilary, and then strolled on giggling, their heads close together. The cognac arrived, poor weak stuff with hardly a kick in it. Hilary sipped it, pulled on his cigarette, sipped the cognac again. He made the cognac last until the cigarette was

finished, and then got up and walked back to the hotel, knowing that it was only half-past nine, telling himself that he'd had a tiring day and a night's rest would do him good.

* * *

In bed, his books and an ashtray ready on the table beside him, he said, Now I must think about it.

For some time he stared at the ceiling, his mind empty. Then he found he was saying, No, I won't think about it to-night, it's too close to me, I'm too tired. To-night I'll just read a little and then I'll go to sleep. He picked up his books and held them up, looking at the backs and wondering which to choose.

Hilary was a fast reader and dreaded nothing more than to be stranded without print. He would read anything sooner than nothing, fragments of sporting news torn up in a lavatory, a motor journal on an hotel table, an out-of-date evening paper picked up in a bus. He would covetously eye the books held by strangers in trains, forcing them into conversation until he could offer his own read book in exchange for something new. But if, by ill-luck, he was reduced to reading nothing but haphazard chance finds that offered his mind only the bare fact of being print, he would become dreary, unhappy, uneasy, like a gourmet who suffers from indigestion after eating bad food.

So he had chosen the books he had brought on this journey principally for their length, good fat books that might annihilate many hours. He held the pile in his hands wondering which to choose. There was a novel by Henry

James, something by Peacock, the Nonesuch Swift, the poems of Clough which Hilary had long been intending to read, and *Dombey and Son*. There was no choice, after all. He picked out *Dombey and Son* and opened it at the death-bed of little Paul.

"'Floy, did I ever see Mamma?'"

"No, darling, why?"

"Did I never see any kind face like a Mamma's looking at me when I was a baby, Floy?'"

Hilary read on, all critical judgment suspended. Little Paul's old nurse came into the sickroom.

"'Is this my old nurse?' said the child,' and Hilary saw imploring black eyes turned to the kindly face and read on:

"'Yes, yes.' No other stranger would have shed those tears at sight of him, and called him her dear boy, her pretty boy, her own poor blighted child. No other woman would have stooped down by his bed and taken up his wasted hand, and put it to her lips and breast, as one who had some right to fondle it. No other woman –'

The book fell on the blanket. Hilary pressed his face into the bolster and sobbed for poor lonely Paul Dombey whose swollen red hands dangled so pitiably from the too short sleeves of his little black overall.

CHAPTER NINE

Tuesday

The next morning Hilary woke at six and with calm detached amusement read Swift until half-past eight.

Then he got up and dressed and as he did so he told himself dispassionately, Yesterday was one hell of a day; it wasn't fair, either on myself or the boy. No one could have made anything constructive out of that ghastly emotional meeting. But now that that's all over, one's got to set about the thing calmly. It's too soon, of course, even to consider whether this is my child or not. One's just got to go gently with him and see what comes out of it.

You can see that direct questions are agonising to the child, he told himself as he cleaned his teeth. It wouldn't be any good badgering him. One's just got to go gently.

Mind you, he said, brushing his hair, he's a nice little boy. Anybody would take to him. He looked at his parting in the glass and found he was smiling tenderly, reluctantly, shame-facedly. He picked up the volume of Swift and took it down to breakfast with him.

Madame was already writing in her little glass pigeon-hole. 'Bonjour, monsieur,' she said curtly as he passed, and

Hilary wished her a sincere 'Good morning,' preferring her sustained hostility to her husband's obsequious smirks.

It seemed that the commercial travellers had already eaten and gone, for the maid was clearing their plates away when Hilary came into the dining-room. 'A *café complet*,' he ordered, and she said with concern, 'There is only bread and ersatz coffee, monsieur, but if monsieur would wish for something more, I can ask the *patron*?' 'No, that will do for me,' said Hilary, rejecting the sullied superior food. But the unbuttered bread was coarse, and dry and hard, and the brown liquid in the cup was unspeakably nauseous, and uneasily he began arguing that *someone* would eat the good food if he didn't, and that he wasn't doing any good by taking up this high-minded attitude.

'Now I must plan my day,' he said.

I've got nothing to do till quarter-past five; well, he demurred, say, till ten past if I walk there slowly. I've got to buy some gloves for Jean. I could get on with my article on Max Jacob – that could take most of the afternoon. I wonder if there's anything to see in this town?

'Mademoiselle,' he called to the maid, 'are there any interesting sights here in A——, anything that tourists go to see?'

She came and stood by his table, her earnest face worried. You could watch her thinking, her mind considering, rejecting, wondering.

'We have not many curiosities in A——,' she said at last. 'There was the Abbey – that was very old, they say, but it was destroyed in the big raid. The Museum too – that went at the same time.' She thought again with obvious effort. 'There's the old castle,' she offered.

'That sounds promising,' commented Hilary. 'Where would I find the old castle?'

'It's rather hard to find,' she said doubtfully, 'and there isn't much of it left. Monsieur knows the road to Boissières?'

'No,' said Hilary regretfully. 'I don't know the district at all.'

'I must think,' said the maid, and lengthily and laboriously proceeded to do so.

At last her face brightened and she said, 'Monsieur must proceed along this street, turn left by the baker's shop and then ask for the house of Madame Mercatel. Everyone knows the house of Madame Mercatel, and the castle is right close by.'

'Mercatel?' said Hilary, interested. 'Is that by any chance the wife of Monsieur Mercatel who teaches at the orphanage?'

'Ah, no, monsieur,' said the maid, 'Madame Mercatel is the mother of Monsieur Bernard. She is a brave woman, is Madame Mercatel. She has suffered greatly.'

'Tell me about her,' said Hilary. He suppressed the memory of his mother's irritable voice telling him that real gentlefolk never gossiped with servants. It's important to me to know about these people, he told himself impatiently.

The maid was only too willing to gossip. Monsieur le Baron, she told Hilary, who had the big château over there – but now it was pulled down – had had five daughters and no sons. Mind you, that was before her time, but her father had been a groom on the estate, and often she had heard her parents talking about it. Monsieur could imagine the difficulty of finding dowries for five daughters – and

Monsieur le Baron had never been a one to stint himself of anything. Monsieur would not credit what she had heard of the splendid parties that used to take place at the château in the old days. Consequently monsieur would not be surprised to hear that when it came to getting the youngest daughter married, Monsieur le Baron was only too glad to accept the offer of Monsieur Mercatel who was wealthy, it was true, but for all that, only a tradesman.

'What was his trade?' Hilary asked.

'He was just a businessman,' the maid said vaguely, 'but three times Mayor of A—— and a greatly respected citizen. And then at the end of the war – the first war, monsieur would understand – well, no one knew quite what had happened but Monsieur Mercatel had lost all his money and shot himself. What a disgrace for the family! What a tragedy for the widow! And poor Monsieur Bernard, who must leave his studies and take to teaching to help to support his mother!'

'Has he been teaching at the orphanage all this time?' Hilary asked.

'All the time,' said the maid with sombre triumph. 'Ah, he is a dutiful son, is Monsieur Bernard. But his mother – there is a magnificent woman. There are few people in this town who cannot tell you of the kindness of Madame Mercatel,' and then without a pause, 'and so monsieur will go and see the castle this morning?'

'No, not this morning,' said Hilary abruptly. He was shy of probing around the home of the man he was to meet later in the day. 'Isn't there anything else to see in A——?' he asked, 'any old churches – or something?'

'There are a few churches,' the maid said doubtfully. It was clear that she had nothing else to suggest, and Hilary dropped his cigarette into his cup, got up and went out.

* * *

First he walked slowly and deliberately round the streets near the hotel, looking critically into each shop-window, comparing the price tickets with the goods displayed, trying to draw sociological deductions, pretending that he was collecting material for an article that he knew he was ill-equipped to write. Then he told himself that he would take the second turn to the left, no matter where that led him, but soon it led him to the hill on the way to the orphanage and he retraced his footsteps back to the centre of the town.

And then he asked a passer-by the way to the nearest church, and having found it, went in, walking slowly past each over-dressed altar, each plaster statue, carefully reading each little framed notice stuck up on the walls. But he could not long pretend that this late nineteenth-century structure had any interest for him, and all too soon he came out into the street.

Then he looked at his watch and it was half-past ten. If I have lunch at twelve, he argued, that's not too far away now to start buying the gloves.

Now he could spin out time looking into the shop-windows again, this time with a different intent. None of the shops seemed to have children's gloves on display, and he was thankful for the excuse to prolong his window-shopping until he had again examined all those in the few narrow streets

that comprised the old part of the town. Then he picked out a small shop he had noticed that showed children's pinafores intermingled with balls of knitting-wool and walked in.

The dark-haired middle-aged woman behind the counter was engrossed in animated conversation with a neighbour with a shopping-basket. Hilary didn't bother to listen. He nodded briefly, and then started to turn over a pile of knitting instructions lying on the counter to show that he was in no hurry, had no impatience to be served.

But Hilary was a potential purchaser and the neighbour only a means of passing the time. As a matter of course the conversation was allowed to flag and die away, and the neighbour moved a little away from the counter to allow the saleswoman to gaze expectantly at Hilary.

'Have you any children's gloves?' he asked.

'For a child of what age?' asked the woman.

'About six,' said Hilary, and the woman pulled out a drawer, slapped it down on the counter before him and said, 'All these are suitable for a child of six.'

'All these' did not, after all, amount to very much. There were a few pairs in a hard grey wool, coarse and prickly to the touch. There was a pair in white rabbit fur, a pair in stripes of mustard and an electric blue. Hilary turned them over dubiously and said, 'What I was really looking for was something gay – bright red, for instance.'

'Wait,' said the woman and pulled out another drawer, 'I believe –' she said, turning its contents over, then, 'Yes, I thought I had a pair. Here, monsieur,' and she pulled out a pair of scarlet knitted gloves.

'Yes, that's the thing,' said Hilary. He took them in his hand and pretended to examine them. 'Are these the same size as those others, madame?' he asked.

The woman said, 'What age, exactly, is the child?'

'Five,' said Hilary, 'well, five and a half.'

'For a child of five and a half those are excellent,' the woman said decisively, and Hilary said, 'I will take them. How much are they?'

The woman took the gloves back and held them consideringly in her hand. 'A hundred francs,' she said. It was not quite a statement, not quite a question, and Hilary protested. 'That's a lot of money for a little pair of gloves.'

But the woman had made up her mind. 'One hundred francs,' she repeated, and Hilary produced a note.

The woman said, 'And the tickets?'

'I don't understand,' said Hilary.

The woman said wearily, 'The gloves are rationed, monsieur.'

'Oh,' said Hilary, 'I didn't know.' The woman began to put the drawers away again and Hilary was left, the limp note hanging from his fingers, protesting to her back, 'You see, I'm English – a visitor. They don't give us tickets. I don't know if there's anything that can be done?'

The woman seemed to ignore him. She turned and spoke in a low voice to the neighbour who shook hands with her and then went out of the shop. Hilary stammered, 'If the gloves are rationed, madame – then I'm afraid –'

She picked up the gloves and wrapped them in a torn piece of white paper. Still not looking at Hilary she said,

'I made a mistake, monsieur. The price of the gloves is one hundred and fifty francs,' and stood waiting, the parcel in her hand.

Slowly, reluctantly, Hilary opened his wallet again and took out another note. I oughtn't to do this, he told himself, but it seems to be the same thing everywhere. Besides it's not for myself – I've got to have the gloves. Then he thought wryly, That's what everyone says, I suppose, that they've got to have it. He found that he wanted to make explanations, to tell the woman that the gloves were for a little orphan, that this Black Market transaction was different from any other, and ashamed, he thrust the parcel into his pocket, said coldly, 'Thank you very much, madame,' and left the shop.

* * *

Still it was only quarter-past eleven. Hilary walked slowly back to the hotel, pretending to interest himself in every poster, every street-name, every chalk *graffito* on every wall. Then he noticed, as he neared the hotel, that on the opposite side of its archway was a café, apparently belonging to the establishment. Thank God, he said, realising gratefully that now there was something other than the bedroom or the street, somewhere he could sit and read or work and perhaps fall into conversation or, at the very least, pass the time in an environment made for that purpose. Mind you, I'd rather not support this particular café, he said, but really, there's no alternative: and neither was there, save the bedroom or the street or the gradual penetration into another café that must be found and deliberately chosen from all

others. No, there was no alternative to the café of the Hôtel d'Angleterre.

So here Hilary passed the rest of the morning. But he brought down his book, and he did not fall into conversation after all. I can't be sure, he told himself, of the people who come here. Probably they're all right, but on the other hand, one would loathe to talk to and perhaps even like someone who had helped the Germans.

And this led him to think again about Pierre who had said that under the Occupation people had done what they must, and that what this was had been settled long before. He thought, Pierre is a better man than I. He has the liberal virtues that I profess and personally lack. I am an intolerant perfectionist; Pierre refrains from judging anyone but himself. And yet I am a liberal intellectual, and Pierre is devoting himself to the furtherance of illiberal perfection. But Pierre can be tolerant of me and I can't be tolerant of him.

Suddenly, he longed for Pierre. If Pierre were here, everything would be all right. If Pierre were here, the boy would be his and perhaps even to-day they would take him and go, leave A—— and the tainted café for ever.

But I mustn't, Hilary told himself, despairingly. I was wrong about Pierre – all right, I know I was wrong about Pierre. I love him and I want him. But I know that I've got to go through this alone.

If Pierre were here, we would agree that Jean is my son. But I wouldn't be sure and I've got to be sure. If I've got to give up my precarious peace, my tentative security, I've got to be sure.

And anyway, he said with relief, the Mother Superior said I must be quite certain. If Pierre were here it would be cheating.

* * *

Then at last it was time for lunch. There was a family party in the dining-room, father, mother, and two whining children, all eating, as Hilary himself ate, hugely of substantial food. And after lunch the sun shone and Hilary took his notebook to a patch of grass he had noticed that morning in a little *place*. He sat on a hard bench and wrote an article which he knew, while he wrote it, was bad, diffuse and useless. But the movement of his pen over the paper at least gave an illusion of activity, and slowly, slowly, the afternoon dragged away.

And at last it was after five o'clock and he was walking up the hill to the orphanage again.

He wondered, as he turned in at the gate, if there was anything new the two of them could do that day. He could take the boy back to the hotel – but he didn't want to, and besides, he reassured himself, there's nothing for him to do there. Should he take him to a restaurant and give him a good meal? He imagined the boy's surprise at the unfamiliar dishes, the delight with which he would eat and eat until he was full – and then thought hurriedly, no, no, it would never do, it wouldn't be right to accustom him to things – but he found he did not wish to follow this argument to any conclusion and uneasily he climbed the steps and rang the bell.

Again Sister Thérèse opened the door, and behind her

voluminous white bulk he could see the white face of the little boy. This time the big eyes were gleaming with radiant excitement. 'Oh, monsieur,' he cried, and he ran forward and shook hands without being told to, and Hilary said good-bye to the nun, and he and the boy went away.

On the steps Jean turned to him a glowing expectant face. Inevitably Hilary smiled and said cheerfully, 'Well, what is it to be to-day?'

Jean breathed rather than said, 'The trains!'

'All right,' agreed Hilary, and this time he took the little boy's hand without thinking about it, and they set off down the hill.

And this time there was no need for Hilary to search desperately for something to say, for the little boy chattered without ceasing. Did monsieur think the goods-train would come again? Did it come from Paris? Robert said he'd seen a passenger-train; perhaps a passenger-train would come this evening. And as he talked his face reflected the eagerness in his voice, and Hilary found this interminable stream of excited chatter not dull but enlivening, rousing him to reply to the questions with a sincere desire to interest as he himself was being interested. He *is* a nice little boy, he said to himself, and when they reached the level crossing, Hilary found that he too was wondering with real interest what train would come first.

They waited this evening until the gates had fallen and risen three times and they saw not only the goods-train but two shunting engines and the longed-for passenger-train, a mean shabby cavalcade of old third-class coaches, but to Jean's ecstatic vision the perfection of locomotion. 'Oh,

monsieur,' he gasped and his hand reached out convulsively and clutched Hilary's raincoat and held on to it tight.

After this the gates went up again and the traffic trickled through and Hilary, looking down the single-track line, could see that the signals reared negative arms. 'I'm afraid there won't be another train for a bit,' he said regretfully, 'shall we go to the café again?'

The boy nodded and followed Hilary to the café, walking without hesitation to the bench he had occupied the previous evening. 'Raspberry syrup again?' Hilary enquired, and began to struggle out of his coat and then remembered the little parcel in his pocket.

He slipped it out surreptitiously under the table and keeping it hidden said, 'Jean, I've got a present for you.'

Jean said incredulously, 'A *present*? For *me*?' His forehead wrinkled into an intense frown and he asked doubtfully, 'Is it my birthday?'

Hilary was reminded of his mission. He said with a forced laugh, 'Now, Jean, you should know when your birthday is better than I do. *Is* your birthday in October?'

The boy looked sadly at Hilary and said, 'I haven't got a birthday.' He seemed to be thinking and then asked, 'Do you think, monsieur, that that's why no one has ever given me a present?'

Hilary said quickly, 'No, of course it isn't. Hardly any boys get presents in wartime, because – because people are busy making guns.' He meant his voice to sound reassuring, but it came out choked with anger. The child looked frightened, but whispered doggedly, 'The other boys have birthdays, and they get presents.'

'Well, anyway,' said Hilary, schooling his voice with an effort to the mysterious gaiety he remembered from present-giving long ago, 'You're getting a present now. Would you like to see what it is?' He brought the parcel up from under the table and held it out to the boy.

Very very slowly Jean's face creased into a wondering smile. He looked at Hilary, looked quickly at the parcel, and then up to Hilary again. Suddenly he put out his hand and snatched the parcel, holding it close to his breast. Then he waited, motionless.

'Go on,' said Hilary, 'open it.'

The boy's smile was of ineffable, incredulous joy. Gently, gradually, still clasping it close to his breast, he plucked the paper from the parcel, and at last the gloves fell out and lay in his lap.

He held the paper and looked at them dreamily as if he feared to break this moment and awake. Hilary found he was biting his lip until it hurt. He made himself relax and said gently, 'Wouldn't you like to try them on?'

The dream was broken. The paper fell on the floor, and Jean had picked up the gloves and was trying urgently, too urgently, to put first one and then the other on his left hand.

'Here, wait a minute,' called Hilary, 'you'll never get them on like that. Let me help you.'

He reached across the table and picked up the hand and a glove. With uneasiness mounting into panic he tried to pull the red ribbing over the red fists, but it was no good; the gloves were too small.

He said nervously, 'I'm afraid it won't do' – and held up the hand, the glove dangling ridiculously on the ends of the fingers.

The boy looked at the glove. He plucked it off, took a glove in each hand, held one fiercely crushed in each fist. Then he burst into tears.

At first doubtfully, and then swiftly and without any doubt, Hilary rose from his seat and went and sat beside the little boy. He put an arm round the heaving shoulders and hugged the child to him, pleading in anguish, 'Don't cry, Jean, please don't. Don't think about those silly old gloves any more.'

Through his sobs the boy shouted, 'They're not silly old gloves,' and Hilary pressed him closer and muttered, 'Don't cry, Jean, please stop crying.'

Gradually the boy's agonised weeping died down. Hilary, bending closely over him, heard him stammer between convulsive sniffs, 'It was my present – they're not silly old gloves.'

'Look, Jean,' Hilary whispered, 'look, couldn't we pretend? Couldn't we pretend that they were your present for your last birthday, when you were still a very little boy? Then we could pretend, you see, that you've just grown out of them and that your real present for this birthday is coming tomorrow?'

Jean opened his fists and gazed sadly at the crumpled gloves. He asked, 'Could I keep them if we pretended that?'

'Why, of course, you could,' Hilary reassured him. 'Don't you see, you'll have two presents instead of one?'

The boy said doubtfully, 'When I grow too big for my clothes, Sister Clothilde gives them to Louis.' Hilary

remembered that his arm was still round the child's shoulders. He withdrew it selfconsciously, and wondered whether to say, 'Then I'll keep them safe for you,' or 'I'll see that they're not given away.' He chose the latter, and then he pulled out his handkerchief and carefully wiped Jean's eyes. 'Blow,' he said, remembering his nursery days, and Jean obediently blew, and then smiled a watery smile.

'And now,' said Hilary, 'what about your raspberry syrup? You won't have time for another one if you're not quick.'

He watched the boy furtively slide the gloves off the table, and crush them up into a little bundle that he held tightly in his left hand. Then he began to drink his syrup and Hilary sipped his beer in silence.

I ought to start questioning him, he was telling himself, but what can I ask him? If he is my son then we met once at the moment of his birth and have had nothing in common ever since. He might tell me what toys he played with – but I have never seen them. He might tell me of other children he knew – but I have never met them. If he remembered being kissed on this particular spot, being put to bed with that particular formula, I would still not know if those were the things that happened between Lisa and my son. I don't even know the little pet names they would have had for each other.

But this gave him an idea. 'Jean,' he said, 'I know your name, but I don't believe you know my name, do you?'

Jean looked up from his syrup and said, 'No, monsieur.'

'My name is Hilary,' said Hilary slowly, watching the boy closely. 'Do you think that is a nice name?'

The boy seemed to weigh the name thoughtfully. 'I think it's quite a nice name,' he answered at last.

'Have you ever heard it before?' asked Hilary.

He could detect no flicker of awareness in the boy's face as he answered, 'No,' and bent to his syrup again.

Hilary tried, 'Which girls' names do you like the best?'

'I don't think I know any girls' names,' said Jean doubtfully.

'Oh, come,' said Hilary with a forced laugh. 'All the sisters have names haven't they? What about Sister Thérèse who opens the door, and Sister Clothilde you were just talking about?'

'Oh, *those* names,' said Jean with comprehension. 'I didn't know those were girls' names. I thought they were just sisters' names.'

'My favourite girl's name is Lisa,' said Hilary.

Jean smiled and said, 'That's a pretty name.'

Hilary demanded urgently, 'Have you ever heard it before?'

Jean shivered, shot a quick glance at Hilary, and whispered, 'No, monsieur.'

Oh, God, said Hilary, now I've frightened him again. He smiled when I said Lisa. Did that mean anything or nothing? It *is* a pretty name – but mightn't he have smiled if I'd said Joyce instead?

I can't go on questioning him, he said in despair, it's agony for both of us and it gets us nowhere. I don't begin to know what to ask him.

Besides, he thought (but didn't say this even to himself) if I go on questioning him I might find out that he was irrevocably *not* my son.

I'll just go on seeing him, he decided, talk to him naturally, try to make friends with him. Surely, if I do that, I shall eventually know.

'Finish up, Jean,' he said, 'it's time we were getting back.'

* * *

'Here he is,' Hilary said to Sister Thérèse, 'safe and sound.'

'And that's a good thing,' said Sister Thérèse, in her rough grumbling voice. 'And there's another thing, monsieur. The front door's always open. There's no need for you to ring the bell each time you come, and fetch me all along the passages to answer it. You just walk in, and if you're coming, Jean will be waiting for you in the hall; if you're going, you can just leave him here and be off. And now,' she turned to the child, 'you run straight up to bed.'

But Jean did not let go of Hilary's hand, only clutched it tightly, desperately. 'What is it?' Hilary asked, bending down, and Jean whispered, 'My present, monsieur. You said you'd ask her.'

'Of course,' said Hilary. 'Ma sœur, I have just given the boy a pair of gloves. Unfortunately these are too small for him. But he likes them so much that he asks if he may keep them for himself just the same.'

'Let's see them,' said the nun. Reluctantly Jean undid his tight fist and delivered the gloves into the big outstretched hand.

'They're good material,' she said grudgingly. 'It seems a wicked waste to let him keep them for nothing when there are other children who could be warm in them.'

'Nevertheless,' said Hilary, 'it is for this child that I have bought them and I must request you to allow him to keep them.'

'And where,' said the nun, 'is he to keep them, may I ask?'

Hilary suggested, 'Well, where does he keep his toys and things?'

'Toys!' said the nun and laughed shortly. 'We haven't any money to spend on toys, monsieur. The boys are here to work.'

Before Hilary's eyes danced the pitiful pile of possessions spread out accusingly on the bed. He said angrily, 'Surely there's some cupboard where you keep his clothes?'

'There is,' said the nun, 'but it's away in the linen room where all the other boys' clothes are kept. I could keep his gloves there for ever and he'd never see them.'

Hilary looked down at the small white face turned so imploringly to his. 'In that case,' he said firmly, 'I will keep the gloves for the boy myself,' and he stepped forward, took them out of Sister Thérèse's hand and stuffed them into his pocket.

'Good-bye, Jean,' he said, 'I'll bring your gloves for you when I come tomorrow,' and he went out of the door and down the steps, filled with an inner panic that he had committed himself to something, he wasn't sure what.

CHAPTER TEN

Tuesday evening

Hilary took his dinner early, propping a book on the table before him to discourage any efforts Monsieur Leblanc might make at conversation. Then he went out into the street and walked up and down. He wanted to avoid the necessity of having Monsieur Mercatel walk into the hotel and show himself to madame, as he asked for Hilary. I don't want everybody knowing my business, he said, and then smiled wryly, thinking what a typically English phrase this was.

But Monsieur Mercatel, when he finally trotted along in a raincoat and grey felt hat, knitted muffler wrapped high round his throat, seemed as relieved as Hilary to meet in the street. 'It is foolish of me,' he admitted, 'but I would feel I had surrendered something if I had to speak to those people, even to ask them a simple question.'

'They really are horrible,' said Hilary with a shiver. 'Where are we going to go?'

Monsieur Mercatel said shyly, 'My mother, monsieur, asks if you would give her the pleasure of coming to our house to take some coffee with us. The cafés here are really not very

nice now – and also, she would very much like to make your acquaintance.'

The suggestion did not appeal to Hilary in the least. He wanted to talk peacefully to this quiet man, not have the strain of making party conversation with an old French-woman renowned for good works. But there was nothing to say except, 'I shall be honoured monsieur; it is extremely kind of your mother,' and they started to walk along the dark silent street.

'You have just come from Paris, have you not?' said Monsieur Mercatel amiably. 'How did you find it there?'

'It remains the most beautiful city in the world,' said Hilary, 'but I found an air of sadness, almost decay about it. One had the impression of a civilisation slowly running down.'

'Yes, it is frightening, that,' Monsieur Mercatel agreed. 'Barbarism is pleasing when it is a primitive state, but not when it is a reversion, when civilisation has gone sour. I don't think I should like to see Paris to-day.'

'It is many years since you've been there?' Hilary asked politely.

'I used to go once a year before the war,' said Monsieur Mercatel, 'to a dinner that was given annually by my colleagues at the Sorbonne. But since the war I haven't been there.'

'You were at the Sorbonne?' said Hilary, doubtful of the status of the colleagues referred to.

Monsieur Mercatel laughed gently without any trace of bitterness. 'I used to teach there,' he explained. 'I was quite

a good mathematician once. I would write very learned theses that would be read by hardly anyone at all. But my old colleagues never forgot me, and it was a great pleasure to go to see them once a year and talk over old times. This year, at last, I hope to go again.'

They walked on a little in silence and then Hilary said from the deep pity he was feeling, 'You must have found it very lonely here all these years.'

'Lonely?' repeated Monsieur Mercatel. He seemed surprised. 'Oh, no, monsieur. You see, I was born here in A—— and went to school here, so I have many good friends in the town. Oh, no, I do not find it lonely here.'

'I mean,' said Hilary, confused by an answer that seemed to him incomprehensible, 'You can't find many people to talk to around here.'

'Aha!' said Monsieur Mercatel, comprehending, 'you mean, to talk to about mathematics. But mathematics is not like literature; it is not a common topic of conversation between friends. No, monsieur, I think about mathematics privately to myself, and then, when I meet my friends, we have everything else in the world to talk about.'

'But –' began Hilary, and stopped. To him it was inconceivable that an intelligent man should be happy to live in a provincial town and talk about everything in the world with people less intelligent than himself. Automatically he found himself deciding that Monsieur Mercatel could not be as intelligent as he had supposed, that he must be a man who was good on his subject and negligible outside it. And yet, he knew I was a poet, he protested confusedly, and at that

moment Monsieur Mercatel said, 'We have a literary society here that meets on the first Tuesday of each month. Last week, one of our colleagues – he is literary critic of our local newspaper – read us a paper on contemporary English literature, and your name was constantly mentioned. Indeed, I was so much interested that I ordered a copy of your poems from Paris, and then two days later you come to see us. Isn't that a strange coincidence?'

'It is, indeed,' said Hilary, 'but you must cancel your order, monsieur, and let me send you a copy myself when I get back to England again.'

'But that is very kind,' said Monsieur Mercatel with evident pleasure, 'I should greatly treasure such a gift.'

The moon was rising over the grey roofs and the stars were shining in the black sky. He is clearly not unintelligent, Hilary was saying to himself as they walked along, but how in God's name can he be happy in this one-eyed town? I should die of boredom if I had to live in the provinces in England. I suppose, he thought resentfully, that he has this capacity for happiness Pierre was talking about. But does that mean, he questioned, that one is able to live anywhere, like people uncritically and just be happy? Yet how could one be happy if one had only fools to talk to? Is he perhaps imbued with the old sentimental belief that the recognition of true worth in anyone makes them a desirable companion on a level of common humanity?

It's a belief that we English intellectuals have totally discarded, he mused. We are bored and resentful if we are expected to be companionable with anyone not of our own

sort – unless, that's to say, he's a left-wing politically conscious tramway-worker. And that, I suppose, is why our work lacks universality; we deliberately encase ourselves in an esoteric coterie and lack the material to generalise about human emotions.

And in the end we lack the material even to feel the emotions ourselves, he was thinking bitterly, and then they turned a corner and Monsieur Mercatel said encouragingly, 'Look, monsieur, here is our home.'

'But how lovely!' said Hilary spontaneously, and delightedly gazed ahead in the moonlight.

There was a short length of road ahead of them that soon turned sharply away to the right. On that side it was bordered by a high wall over which he could dimly see the shape of huge bare branches. Ahead, on the bend of the road, the ruined castle reared its tattered battlements, and through its empty windows the stars shone beyond. To the left was a cluster of old houses, each different and each enchanting. There was a long low house traced with beams more tenuous than ever in England, another long but higher house with a plastered front, windows adorned with little low hedges in wooden boxes, and next to that, close up to the turn of the road, a small eighteenth-century house of great simplicity and exquisite proportions.

'This is delightful,' said Hilary, not trying to conceal his surprise. 'I had completely given up hope of finding anything beautiful in this town.'

'There are still a few things saved from the ravages of the present,' said Monsieur Mercatel. 'People think our northern

towns ugly, but you will often find such a corner as this that no one has remembered to bomb or to pull down – though never on the main roads where the tourists go.' He led the way to the middle house with the little box hedges at the windows, pulled an enormous key out of his pocket and inserted it in a massive old lock.

Inside they were in a small tunnel, the house rising on all sides of them. 'This way,' said Monsieur Mercatel, turning to a door on the left, and as they went he explained, 'we used to have the whole house, but of late years, when there has been only my mother and myself, this wasn't necessary. So now we do very well with an *appartement* on the ground floor, and the rest of the house is let off.'

'Very convenient,' said Hilary politely, guessing that only need would have enforced such an arrangement. They passed down a grey-painted passage and then Monsieur Mercatel opened a door and stood back for Hilary to pass through.

He was in a room so lovely that it made him catch his breath in surprised amazement. It was a large room, once evidently the *salon* of a house built for spacious formality. Its three long windows were hung with heavy yellow silk, its walls covered with toile de Jouy, upon which delicately etched grey gallants and their ladies cavorted in mock rusticity. At the end of the room stood an enormous rose-wood bookcase; against the middle window a little painted spinet; then Hilary's eye travelled down the room, and beside a massive fireplace where a log fire was burning he saw his hostess sitting in an upright rosewood chair, and he moved towards her.

She said in perfect English, 'I am delighted that you have come, Mr. Wainwright. You will forgive me if I do not rise to greet you, but I am crippled with arthritis.'

'*Mais, madame –*' said Hilary, utterly astounded. Then he remembered his manners and shook hands, and then he said in English, 'You must forgive my surprise. But please will you tell me how you come to speak my language so perfectly?'

She was a little crumpled bundle of an old lady, dressed in a shabby old-fashioned black frock, a lace scarf yellow with age over her scanty white hair. She seemed immeasurably old and frail, and entirely and irrevocably un-English.

Now she said in the voice Hilary had heard so often among the old ladies of the Cathedral Close, 'I must confess, Mr. Wainwright, that I had hoped to surprise you. But the explanation is very simple. My mother was English, and when I was a girl' – she said 'gel' – 'we used to go every year to stay with my grandparents in Holland Park.'

'Have you been in England lately?' asked Hilary stupidly, still not recovered from his surprise.

'Not for nearly forty years,' said Madame Mercatel. 'My grandparents died shortly before the last war, and gradually we lost touch, although such of my cousins as are left alive still write to me and occasionally send me a welcome parcel. But come and sit down, Mr. Wainwright. I am sure you are cold after your walk.'

Hilary sat in a rosewood chair with a great brass eagle bestraddling the back. 'How nice to see an open fire,' he said tritely.

Madame Mercatel laughed. 'When I married, I said to my husband that at last I had an English fireplace of my own, and I well remember how he laughed at me for, of course, one finds open fireplaces in many old French houses. And, indeed, we have all found it very pleasant, and particularly now, for central-heating furnaces take unkindly to wood and if it were not for my open fire we would often have been frozen.' She turned to her son and said, 'Bernard, will you pour out the coffee. My hands,' she said ruefully to Hilary, 'can no longer be trusted with the proper duties of a hostess.'

From a side table Monsieur Mercatel handed round coffee in tiny paper-thin Chinese cups, and thin slices of sugared sponge-cake. 'It is real coffee,' said Madame Mercatel, 'it came in one of my English parcels, and I saved it for just such an occasion.'

'It is extremely good,' said Hilary appreciatively, 'but you shouldn't have wasted your precious coffee on me.'

'Nonsense,' said the old lady vigorously. 'You don't know what a treat it is for me to talk English again. I was beginning to think I would forget it completely.'

'Do you speak English, too, monsieur?' asked Hilary politely.

Monsieur Mercatel said, 'I can understand it very well, but I cannot talk it with ease. So, if you will forgive me, I will continue to speak French. It will be a queer conversation, perhaps, but I know it will give my mother such pleasure to talk English.'

'It is a great pleasure to me, too,' said Hilary truthfully. It was more than a pleasure; it was an immeasurable relief.

It was not until now that he appreciated how much greater had been the strain of these last days because he must always be speaking in a language not his own, must always before he used a word, pause to weigh it and wonder how exact a synonym it was for his thought. Now, the relief of being able to talk without this continuous process of consideration, of translating imperfectly, not only his thoughts, but thereby his very personality, gave him a sense of being himself as he had not been since he left England.

'What a lovely room this is, madame,' he said, feeling himself warm and unfold to its beauty.

'Yes,' she said, 'the proportions are excellent, but of course all the furnishings are very old-fashioned. When I married, I wanted my husband to get everything new for me, but on that point he was adamant. "You have got your English fireplace," I remember him saying, "and you must be content with that. It would be a sin to replace all this good stuff. When my grandfather bought it, he meant it to last a hundred years and so it will." And I couldn't move him. But I have got used to it now.'

Hilary noticed that she was perfectly serious, and wondered what kind of furniture she had begged her husband to install instead of this lovely Empire stuff. Probably mid-Victorian Holland Park, he thought amusedly, and as if to chime with his thought she said at that moment, 'And now, Mr. Wainwright, please tell me about London. I suppose I would hardly know my Holland Park now. Has it suffered much from the bombing?'

Hilary set himself out to charm. Consciously he adapted

himself to her outlook and period, using his words as carefully, as pedantically as he believed they were used by the writers she would have admired. Thus he talked to her about London during and after the war, about English manners and customs, about changing tastes and appearances, remembering always to relate what he said to what she would have known. Gradually he allowed her comments to monopolise more and more of the conversation, listening with the precious delight of a connoisseur while she came to talk of Grandpapa who was a tea-broker, 'but they were a very literary family for all that, always interested in the new writers of the period,' of her cousin Alice who had been the artistic one and had once brought home a book illustrated by Mr. Aubrey Beardsley 'and Grandpapa put it straight on to the fire and no one dared say a word,' and of Guy, 'he was such a jolly fellow, Mr. Wainwright, always a laugh and a quip for everyone,' but who had gallantly died, alas, in the Second Matabele War. The dim lights flickered uneasily as she talked, Monsieur Mercatel sat in his chair with an expression of relaxed content and Hilary listened, consciously savouring the knowledge that here, for this moment, he knew enjoyment and was free and happy.

The old lady's talk died away and for a while they sat quietly like old friends who can afford silence, listening only to the small green logs spluttering on the hearth. Hilary sighed. Madame Mercatel echoed his sigh, then asked, 'What do you think of France now, Mr. Wainwright?'

Hilary answered truthfully as he would not have done if they had been speaking French, 'I think it is horrible

– horrible and desperately unhappy. I used to love and admire France more than any country I knew, but coming back to it now, I find it enveloped in a miasma of corruption.'

Monsieur Mercatel nodded gravely. His mother said, 'To me, the most horrible thing is hearing everyone excusing themselves on the ground that deceit was started against the Germans and has now become a habit. It would have been better to have been honest, even with Germans, than to end by deceiving each other and finally by deceiving ourselves.'

Monsieur Mercatel spoke for the first time since the conversation had begun between his mother and Hilary. He said in French, 'I am not sure that we really deceive ourselves. I think we pretend this and that because we must be ashamed of so many things, even of the truth.'

Madame Mercatel continued to speak in English. She said vigorously, 'And what could be worse than that, that French people should be ashamed of the truth? Do you know what the smart war-time fashions of Paris were like, Mr. Wainwright?'

'Well, I've seen some illustrations –' said Hilary, puzzled.

'We were told,' she said, 'that those fashions were designed as a gesture of defiance, to anger the Germans by displaying to them handsome females they could not have. When I was a young woman,' she said sternly, 'there was a word for women who wore clothes for this purpose – and believe me, Mr. Wainwright, it was *not* "member of the Resistance."'

'But, maman –' began Monsieur Mercatel. His mother raised a hand to silence him. 'We must look facts in the face,' she said, 'I may say this in English, but I am Frenchwoman

enough to believe it is true.' She looked at Hilary and asked, 'Do you look facts in the face, Mr. Wainwright?'

'I try to,' said Hilary, wondering what should be his honest answer to this question, 'but I am so seldom certain of the facts.' He thought what a gulf lay between himself and his hostess who had never doubted them.

She said, 'I am so interested that you have come about the child Jean. It was I, you know, who persuaded the Mother Superior to take him in.'

'No!' said Hilary, interested. 'I didn't know that.'

'I was with her, discussing some business, when the old washerwoman came with the child,' she explained. 'At first the Mother Superior doubted whether she could take him. Their rules of admittance are strict, as you can imagine. But I have a certain influence with her – I organise a committee of ladies in this town who collect money and clothes for the orphanage – and I persuaded her that this was a case where we might properly stretch the rules a little.'

'Why did you do that?' Hilary asked.

'I have often wondered about it,' she answered. 'I am not naturally sentimental about children; this is one of the reasons why the Mother Superior and I can work so well together, for she is not a sentimental woman either. No, for some reason I felt a personal sense of pity for this child such as I have not felt for any of the others.'

'He *is* a pitiable little object,' said Hilary tenderly.

She smiled. 'Ah, you feel it too,' she said, 'and I wonder whether you share the other rather strange feeling I had about this boy – that here was a child it could give one great

happiness to help?' She peered intently at him, shading her eyes with a frail yellow hand on which the mauve veins stood out in swollen relief. But Hilary's face showed none of the sudden comprehension and hope he had felt at her words, and she let her hand fall into her lap again and added gently, 'And have you any idea whether he is your son, Mr. Wainwright?'

Hilary thought with surprise, I ought to resent this question, and coldly ward off this intrusion of my privacy. And yet I want to talk about it, here and now and to these people. I want to talk about it in my own language to this woman who is the one with whom I should have always been able to discuss it, even before I came, back in the tawdry white house in the London suburb, back in the old red-brick house by the Cathedral Close. He wondered swiftly, Will she tell me what I ought to do? and then he answered her. 'I don't know if he is my son,' he said. 'There is nothing about him that tells me whether he is or whether he isn't.' To himself he added, I don't even know whether I want him to be.

Monsieur Mercatel said, 'I have been wanting to tell you, monsieur, speaking as his schoolmaster, what I think of the boy. Whether he is your son or not, of course I cannot say. What I can say, is that he is certainly the son of someone like you.'

'What do you mean?' Hilary asked.

'He is of a mental calibre quite different from the other boys,' said Monsieur Mercatel. 'Mind you, I am not saying that he could be a brilliant scholar – it is too early for judgments of that sort. But I have been teaching these orphans

for many years now, and never before have I had one of whom I could certainly say that he came from a cultured and intellectual background. Little Jean has a mental agility – a sense of causation, perhaps we should say – that is different in kind from the intellects of the other children with whom I have to deal.'

Listening to him, Hilary had felt a sense of pride. If this is my son, then I needn't be ashamed, he thought, but he argued, 'Of course, it is more than probable that a child concealed as this one was would be from a family of intellectuals. After all, those were the people most likely to get into trouble with the Germans.'

'That, of course, is true,' Monsieur Mercatel admitted. His mother asked, 'And what about the physical appearance of the child, Mr. Wainwright. Can you trace any likenesses there?'

'I can't,' said Hilary, almost desperately. 'I'm quite sure he's nothing like my wife.'

Madame Mercatel said, 'Do you carry a photograph of her?'

The little photograph that Hilary carried in the back of his wallet had been taken by an Oxford friend who had come to visit them in Paris. This was in the days when young men interested in photography vied in making portraits that were each more fantastically dramatic than the one before. The subject was stretched out on the floor, glimpsed peeping behind a skull, seen through a glass of champagne, and always with a background of inky blackness. By those standards, Hilary's photograph was comparatively conventional, and yet he was extremely reluctant to show it to Madame

Mercatel. Slowly pulling out his wallet he remembered the face in the picture, the play of light and shadow that emphasised the smooth shining hair and the high cheek-bones cradled in long pointed fingers; it was a long way from the conventional portrait of a conventional Victorian wife. More, he remembered the expression on Lisa's face, her long slanting eyes gazing away from the camera with brooding intensity. This was how he had known her face, when, his passion spent, he had lain on the bed and seen her looking down at him. He had said to her once, 'Now I know what Blake meant by "the lineaments of gratified desire",' and pulling out the photograph and looking at it again, it seemed to him that there could be no other interpretation of that face. Frowning slightly, he handed it to Madame Mercatel.

She held it close to her eyes and peered at it for a few moments. 'Your wife was a very beautiful woman,' she told Hilary. 'I suppose this was taken after the baby was born?'

'Why should you say that?' he asked, startled.

'The expression on the face,' she said. 'One can see that this is a woman of a truly maternal nature.' She sighed and laid the photograph in her lap. 'What a tragedy!' she said.

'Do you mind if I see it?' asked Monsieur Mercatel.

'No, of course not,' said Hilary. What a queer mistake, he was thinking, and then, wildly – or was it a mistake? To avoid thinking about it further he said, 'You see – there's no likeness between my wife and this boy.'

'Oh, no, none at all,' agreed Madame Mercatel. 'It is rather you whom the boy resembles.'

Hilary stammered, 'Do you mean you think he's actually like me?'

Madame Mercatel spoke slowly and carefully. 'I do not for one minute mean to say that there is such a likeness that anyone seeing the boy and then meeting you would immediately know that he was your child. My son looked for such a likeness when he first met you; he did not find it and neither do I. But I would say that there is sufficient resemblance to make it not improbable that he is yours. Do you agree, Bernard?' She turned to her son, who said, 'Yes, I do agree. There is nothing one can put one's finger on, but the general impression is that some likeness is there.'

Hilary said confusedly, 'I hadn't really thought much of his looking like me. I can see that superficially we're not unalike – we've both got the same colour hair, the same sort of thin build –' He broke off, trying in his memory to translate the unformed childish nose, the pale lips into recognisable adult form.

'You both have hair that grows to a point in the neck,' said Monsieur Mercatel.

'But the eyes,' said Hilary pleadingly, 'think of the boy's enormous dark eyes. Neither my wife nor I has – had eyes like that.'

'And you know of no such eyes in your family?' asked Madame Mercatel. He had the impression that they waited like judges for his reply.

He thought of his mother, his father, Uncle Jim and his sister Eileen. 'No,' he said, 'there are no eyes like that in my family,' and then he thought of something and added slowly,

'As a matter of fact, I've just remembered that Lisa's – my wife's Polish aunts had very big dark eyes.'

They both nodded gravely. He had made the right answer. He begged, 'But all that's nothing to go by, is it? I mean, there's nothing definite there. You can trace resemblances in anyone if you consider the whole of their families.'

'No,' said Madame Mercatel, 'there is no evidence there that you need consider conclusive.'

He had been wrong. The judges were not favourable after all.

He replaced the photograph carefully in his wallet, and said, 'It really is time for me to be getting back to the hotel. I must thank you for a most delightful evening.'

'The pleasure was mine,' said Madame Mercatel formally. 'I hope you will come and see me again before you go. How much longer are you going to stay in A——?'

'I don't know yet,' said Hilary, standing up. 'But I should be delighted to come again if you will ask me.'

She smiled graciously. Monsieur Mercatel said, 'I will see you back to your hotel.'

'No, please don't trouble,' insisted Hilary, and at last persuaded them to let him go alone.

At the great door into the street Monsieur Mercatel said, 'I was so happy to see what pleasure it gave my mother to talk with an Englishman again.'

'It was a great privilege to meet her,' said Hilary, and knew that despite the intolerable life in the provincial town he bitterly and resentfully envied Monsieur Mercatel.

CHAPTER ELEVEN

Wednesday

The next morning it was raining steadily and heavily out of a dark grey leaden sky. There could be no question of sauntering round the town, of pretending to choose to walk this way rather than that, till the hours had ebbed away. Hilary was squandering his books too quickly at mealtimes when he read to ensure privacy; to give up the morning to reading would leave the afternoon entirely empty.

But there was nothing else to do. For some time he read in the deserted café, waving aside the bullet-headed porter who acted as barman as well as apparently doing all the odd jobs in the hotel. Hilary thought this man, whom the regular clients called Lucien, was mentally deficient. He seldom spoke, only came at intervals to stand beside Hilary's chair and silently stare down at his book, and while he did so Hilary could not read, could only sit tensely hunching his shoulders, irrationally afraid that the man was going to touch him. At last he could stand it no longer and went up to his bedroom to lie on his bed and read as slowly as he could until it was time for lunch.

After lunch the rain was still pouring down. He had saved for the afternoon the need for buying the new pair of gloves and welcomed this necessary excursion as though it were a long promised treat. He came down the stairs in his trench-coat, the collar turned up tightly round his ears, and found at the bottom the little old servant who said anxiously, 'Monsieur is surely never going out in this!'

'I must,' said Hilary, smiling at her worry. She said, 'Ah yes, monsieur le patron told us of the poor little child that monsieur has come to see.'

Hilary said furiously, 'Monsieur le patron would do well to mind his own business and so would everyone else.' Then he noticed that she was trembling and forced himself to say more gently, 'You know, English people hate to have their business discussed.' 'Yes, of course, monsieur,' she said timidly and then, as he moved away from her, 'Monsieur – I do not wish to offend but – if monsieur must go out in the rain, I can lend him my umbrella.'

The last thing Hilary wanted was an umbrella, but he turned back and said appreciatively, 'How very kind of you. I should be most grateful.' She scuttled off and came back with a huge cotton umbrella which she presented to him proudly.

'Thank you,' he said, and as an afterthought, 'May I ask your name?'

'Mariette, monsieur,' she said, and he said, 'Thank you, Mariette,' and went out in the rain, past madame's cold, sneering face, with the big cotton umbrella.

* * *

He took the umbrella with him when later that afternoon he walked up the hill to the orphanage. There'll be no looking at trains this afternoon, he thought, the best thing we can do is to go straight to the café and get out of the wet, and he knew that he was disappointed, that he had looked forward to the frenzied clutch on his coat, the breathless ecstatic voice whispering, 'Look, monsieur, the train!'

He opened the door this time and walked straight in. Jean was sitting waiting on a bench by the wall in his little black overall. He jumped up as Hilary came in, and this time he grinned with a cheerful friendly completely natural little boy's grin.

'Where's your coat?' asked Hilary, 'You'll want to do it up tightly this nasty wet day.' Damn, he thought, I'm talking like an old nanny already.

'Sister Thérèse said I was to tell her when you came,' said Jean, and clattered off down the corridor.

He came back, the old nun shuffling behind him. 'Good afternoon, monsieur,' she said, 'the Mother Superior said that if you came, you could use the reception room until half-past seven, seeing what the weather's like.' She turned the handle and flung the door open, and brusquely went away down the corridor.

What does she mean by 'if I came'? thought Hilary resentfully. Does she think I'm the sort of person to neglect my duty because of the bad weather? All these people seem to set up a standard and then stand back to see how one measures up to it, he thought, and said, 'Well, come along, Jean. We'll be dry here, at all events.'

Entering the room it was impossible not to remember the last time he had been in it. He went up to the window and stared out over the red and green hexagons, feeling wearily unhappy and drained of all vitality.

The boy stood silently behind him. At last Hilary turned round and smiled and Jean, as though he had been waiting for this signal, burst out, 'Did you bring my present?'

Hilary knew that it was not the new gloves that were meant. Slowly, mysteriously, he fished in the pocket of his coat, and after tremendous exploratory fumblings triumphantly brought out the crumpled red gloves.

Jean sighed ecstatically and took them in his hand. 'They *are* beautiful, aren't they?' he said, as one stating a fact about which there could be no possible disagreement.

'Well,' said Hilary briskly, 'what are we going to do?' He looked round the room, but there was no help there. 'We'll sit down at the table,' he decided, 'and then perhaps we could play a game. Do you know any games?'

Jean shook his head, but obediently climbed on to one of the hard chairs and Hilary sat down beside him.

'I'll show you a game I used to play when I was a little boy,' he said and pulled from his pocket a notebook and pencil, and began making dots in a square on the lined page.

He glanced up to notice that beside him Jean was absorbedly and methodically picking his nose. He raised a hand to knock down the questing fingers, and then stopped himself. I've got no right, he said, I've got no right. Deliberately he told himself, One can't go about disciplining other people's children.

'Look, Jean,' he said, 'this is how we play.'

Carefully he explained the game to the child, delighted at the alacrity with which he picked up the simple rules. They played once, Hilary avoiding opportunities so that the child should win, which he did with rapturous delight. But towards the end of the second game, Jean began to miss obvious chances of scoring and at last Hilary said sharply, 'Don't be stupid, Jean. Surely you can see that if you join those two dots, you'll have another box.'

'But I wanted *you* to win this time,' said Jean, looking hopefully in Hilary's face. Hilary must understand that it was not stupidity but the wish to give that was holding him back. He accepted the gift, and, this conceded, Jean played the third and fourth games with surprising skill.

But Hilary was now bored with Boxes. 'Would you like to see your new gloves?' he asked, and Jean said, Yes, he would, but without very much interest.

The new gloves were of dark grey wool, all that Hilary had been able to find. Jean said, 'Thank you,' and docilely allowed Hilary to show him how well they fitted, but these were valueless compared with the too-small red ones which he held, all the time, tightly clutched in his left hand.

Hilary, peeping surreptitiously at his watch, saw that it was still only quarter-past six. He thought back over his own childhood, wondering how he had then filled wet afternoons, but could think only of painting and jig-saws and meccano and picture-books, all occupations that presupposed a tended child that had received many presents. Then he remembered something else and suggested, 'Shall I tell you a story?'

'Oh, *yes*,' said Jean emphatically. Hilary asked jealously, 'Who else tells you stories?' 'Sister Clothilde tells us about the little saints,' Jean explained. 'I love stories.' His face was shining with expectant delight.

'I don't know any stories about little saints,' said Hilary, trying hard to remember what he himself had enjoyed when he was five. I have a horrible feeling it was Winnie-the-Pooh, he thought, but I'm damned if I'm going to introduce any child to that type of whimsicality. He started to wonder how far a parent could be justified in refusing to allow his child pictures or writings that he as an adult must condemn on aesthetic grounds – and was recalled by Jean pulling at his sleeve and urging, 'Please do begin.'

With sudden relief Hilary remembered Little Red Riding Hood. 'Once upon a time,' he began, 'there was a little girl –' and as he told the story they looked into each other's eyes, both of them absorbed in the story and in each other.

Jean was an admirable child to tell stories to. He was obviously and palpably enthralled. His big eyes widened at each apprehension, at the climax his hand reached out blindly to clutch Hilary's sleeve, and even when the story was finished he still sat motionless, staring thoughtfully at Hilary.

'What do you think of the story?' Hilary asked.

'Monsieur,' said Jean, 'did the little girl's father love her?'

'Oh, yes,' said Hilary with assurance.

'And her mother?'

'Certainly,' said Hilary.

'Then why,' said Jean, his forehead wrinkled, 'did they let her go and meet the wolf?'

'But they didn't know she was going to meet the wolf,' said Hilary, pleased at this evidence that the child had followed the story intelligently, 'and her father came and saved her from the wolf, and then he took her safely home to her mother.'

Jean looked down at the table and then slyly, slantingly up at Hilary, 'Do my father and mother love me?' he demanded.

'Why, of course,' said Hilary in distress.

He flung up his head and stared at Hilary who did not, could not answer. They stared at each other, each with a separate agony, and then the little boy dropped his eyes to the table again.

I could say it now, Hilary thought, I could say it now.

Jean said, still looking at the table, 'Do you know Armand?'

'No,' said Hilary, 'who's Armand?'

Jean said quickly, 'One day Sister Thérèse came into the classroom and she fetched Armand and there was a man waiting and he was Armand's father back from the war and he took Armand away with him.' He stole the same sly sideways glance at Hilary and swiftly looked down again. He said, 'Luc's father came back from Germany and Luc went away, too.'

Oh, God, cried Hilary, oh, my God. Has someone been talking to him or has he just worked it out for himself? Maybe there's nothing in it, maybe he's just making party conversation. Damn that old woman last night, he thought, it's not fair. I don't know yet. I won't be committed. Already I've been forced to feel pity deeper than anything I dreamt I could feel.

I daren't let it go any further – not yet. He stood up and said, 'Jean, I've got to go now.'

Jean demanded rather than asked, 'You're coming tomorrow?'

'If I can,' said Hilary.

'You take my red gloves,' said Jean urgently, and Hilary blindly took the gloves, thrust them into his pocket and went away.

* * *

I am being destroyed, said Hilary as he trudged back in the rain. I know my duty. I came here prepared to do my duty. If the child were mine, I'd take him; if he weren't, I'd leave him. It was to be as simple as that. There was to be no place for feeling in such a decision. Duty must still be the operative word, not feeling.

I must be sure for Lisa's sake. It was my child she wanted me to save, our child, the child of our love. I have no duty to save a pitiable orphan who is nothing to me.

I must guard myself against emotion. I must not let myself be destroyed again, no, not even if the child is mine.

But if the child is mine I must take him for Lisa, who wanted me to save our child even more than she wanted to live. With sudden jealousy he demanded, Did she love the child more than she loved me?

I knew her as my mistress, he thought, I never knew her as the mother of my child. Did she find, when he was born, that a new range of emotions was born with him so that she could find ultimate happiness in cherishing him?

But she cherished *me*, he cried, and again the jealousy pierced him. She gave everything to me and I to her.

And how can I give now when I want so much to be given?

I could give to Lisa. Ours was a perfect relationship, each giving, each taking, in proper proportion.

Then he remembered Madame Mercatel as she gazed at Lisa's picture. Did I give? he wondered wildly, Did I give? Was I ever capable of giving?

It was a perfect relationship, he repeated desperately, each giving, each taking. What the hell did that woman mean by Lisa's maternal expression? It wasn't a maternal expression. It was gratified desire. I was so utterly happy then. It must have been gratified desire.

CHAPTER TWELVE

Thursday and Friday

Thursday morning was different because Hilary, having the night before finished everything he had brought to read, unexpectedly found a stationer's shop with a shelf of books for sale, and was thus able to spend half-an-hour turning them over and pretending to decide which he would have. In fact there was very little choice, and eventually, having glanced through a pile of thrillers and romances obviously so banal as to be almost unreadable, he came away with a novel by Daudet he had never heard of.

At lunch Mariette told him with pride that this evening the cinema would be open. He felt an obligation to this timid old woman; by responding kindly to her, he could feel he was justifying his avoidance of the horrible *patron* and his wife. 'How very nice,' he said, forcing a grateful enthusiasm, and then realised that he was indeed grateful, that here was one evening when a precious book need not be consumed in the unutterable tedium of the dreary café.

At half-past five he was at the orphanage and then he and Jean walked down to the level-crossing, into the café and back up the hill again.

For all his misery and resentment those two hours were different from the rest of his intolerable days. For these two hours he must be sensitive, not to himself and his own reactions, but to the child. He must hide his fear and his boredom, must strive to interest and amuse. And he must try constantly now to keep the meeting gay and secure and never to open a breach through which emotion could suddenly flood in.

More, he enjoyed the child's company. It was clear that Jean had no great reserves of energy; after a burst of movement or excited chatter, he would grow quiet and sit silent with his huge eyes fixed on Hilary and his red gloves inseparably clasped in his hand. But under Hilary's constant efforts he showed himself a gay little boy and even, at times, a witty little boy.

Hilary found he was worried by the physical state revealed by the child's need for periods of rest and withdrawal. He thought that the boy was the wrong type for community life with its constant demands upon the individual vitality. He ought to be on a farm, he thought, carefully avoiding the definite article, where he could be free to run about till he was tired and flop down whenever he felt like it. He tried to imagine the boy in dungarees and a pullover, tidy and rosy-cheeked, and then hurriedly checked his imagination, thought of yet another joke to make the little boy laugh.

Without question, this evening, he held out his hand for the red gloves before he went away.

* * *

In the evening he went to the cinema. The performance had started while he was still eating his dinner, and when he

171

arrived it was already the interval, that interminable interval of French cinemas, enlivened only by the local tradesmen's lantern-slides advertising their wares. But at last the lights went down, and the big film began.

There was no knowing when this film had been made. The spots and cracks and flickers in the celluloid suggested a generation of travelling in battered canisters from one provincial town to another to be shown in little ramshackle cinemas open for one night in a week. In this one the amplifier was too strong, and the sound-track, already sadly worn, was reproduced in noise so loud and distorted that only occasionally could Hilary understand what was being said. But there was little need to strain to understand, for the story was of the most banal and obvious kind. There was a railwayman who had a black-haired daughter. There was an honest peasant lover. There was a city slicker. Through all the permutations of lust and violence, betrayal and destruction, he could smell the strong cheap perfume of the woman beside him so that the two things, the film and the perfume, became interwoven with each other.

Thus, despite his distaste for the vulgarity of the perfume and the vulgarity of the film, his senses gradually became stirred. Both the film and the perfume had been manu-factured on the assumption that sexual desire was a potent force and that people could choose to lead lives in which the satisfaction of that desire was the driving motive. And as he sat there, lonely in the dark, there was roused in him, not sexual desire itself, but a half-formulated wish that some passion as compelling as he had known sexual desire to be

should sweep him from barrenness to emotion urgent and then satisfied. There was some barrier that must be forced, some ordeal that must be endured –. The film ended and the lights went on, and still he had not managed to discover what this emotion of release could be.

* * *

On Friday morning he visited the stationer again and bought a detective story.

On Friday afternoon he shut himself in his bedroom and struggled with a chapter for a book of criticism he had been writing before he left England.

The air was close and heavy this day as if there was going to be a thunderstorm, and walking up the hill he was oppressed with an uneasy restlessness. He had no longer any volition about his days; deliberately unthinking he had let them fall away, neither greeting nor resenting the familiar routine. Only this evening, his skin pricking with the imminent thunder, he felt that somebody must soon make something happen for him, must lift the net that now so inextricably held him enmeshed.

* * *

Then, when he took the boy back into the hall again, Sister Thérèse was waiting.

'The Mother Superior would like to see you,' she said dourly, and Hilary, an apprehensive sinking at his heart, followed her.

Again the Mother Superior was seated behind her desk.

'Thank you for coming, monsieur,' she said, and motioned Hilary to a chair as Sister Thérèse went out of the room.

'I'm afraid Sister Thérèse doesn't like me very much,' Hilary said with an uneasy laugh.

The Mother Superior looked up as if interrupted in a train of thought. Then she politely echoed Hilary's laugh and said, 'No, it is not that she dislikes you. She is jealous.'

'Jealous?' repeated Hilary. 'Do you mean she's jealous about Jean?'

The nun's brow was puckered as if trying to explain motives was an unaccustomed and difficult task. 'No, I don't think it is exactly that,' she said, 'but in looking after children as we do, one is apt to become fond of them, not individually, but as a whole. So when one child is singled out for attention, as Jean has been this past week, there is a tendency to resent it on behalf of the others.'

'I hope she hasn't been taking it out on him,' said Hilary uneasily.

'Oh, no,' said the nun, shocked. 'Sister Thérèse is a very good woman.'

She fiddled with her rosary, as if unwilling to broach the real object of this interview, and then said with sudden relief, 'Oh, before I forget, I have a message for you from Monsieur Mercatel. He fears that you will be thinking him very neglectful of you, but for the last few days his mother has been confined to her bed, and as their maid goes home in the evenings, he naturally could not leave her.'

'I hope it is nothing serious,' said Hilary, relieved to know that he was excused from facing again the tribunal before which he felt he had condemned himself.

'It is only her arthritis,' said the Mother Superior, 'the wet weather often prostrates her. Monsieur Mercatel asks me to add that they both hope to see you again before you go.' She paused, while her fingers again played with her beads. Then she said, 'That brings me to what I want to say. Since you have not yet come to tell me anything, I understand that you have been unable to reach a decision about the little Jean, that you still do not know whether he is your lost son.'

'That is true, ma mère,' answered Hilary.

'You remember,' she said, 'that when you first came to see me I told you that you must be very sure about your decision, because you were not a Catholic, and you informed me that in any case your son would be brought up as a Catholic? That is so, is it not?'

'Yes,' said Hilary.

'Since then,' said the nun, 'I have thought much about it. I have asked the advice of Father Ludovic, who is our Confessor and a very good man, and also I have continually prayed for guidance.' She bent her head, and Hilary thought with surprise that for the first time since he met her he saw her as a religious rather than a hospital sister. 'I am convinced that it is right that you should take this child.'

'Even if he is not my son?' asked Hilary incredulously.

'Listen, monsieur,' said the nun, 'if you do not know whether this child is yours or not, how will you ever know with any child? Your instinct has told you nothing, or you would be sure, one way or the other. I am certain that you have questioned him and have tried to find out all he remembers, and, as one expected, he has remembered nothing that could help you. If this is not your child, if your own child is still waiting

175

to be found, you will still never know whether another child is yours or not.'

Hilary said, 'Another child might really remember something. Or it might look so like my wife that I couldn't help but be sure.'

'Time is passing,' said the nun, 'a child forgets a little more every day. No other child would remember more than this one does of what happened three years ago. And as for a resemblance – I do not know about your wife, but it is certain that little Jean is not unlike you.'

Hilary said vehemently, 'I couldn't bear to take the wrong child and then perhaps find my own later on.'

'But you will not,' said the nun, 'that is as nearly certain as anything can be. If this child is not yours, then you will never find your son.'

Unthinkingly Hilary said, 'That's just what Pierre said.'

'Pierre?' she questioned.

'My friend, Monsieur Verdier,' Hilary explained. 'The one who first wrote to you.'

'Oh, yes,' she said, 'I understood from his letter that he had already made a most exhaustive search for your son, and that this child that we have here was the only probable one he had discovered. No, monsieur, I am sure that either this is your son, or that your son is beyond human reach. And since I am assured that he would be brought up in the faith, I should be very content if you wished to recognise this child as yours.'

'Why?' asked Hilary sharply, 'Why are you so anxious that I should take him?'

She looked at him steadily for a moment and then said,
'There are many reasons. One is that I am deeply sorry for
you. You seem to me lost and in need of comfort. I would not
wish to withhold that comfort from you.'

Hilary whispered stupidly, 'I don't want anyone to be sorry
for me,' and knew for an instant that he did, that he wanted
that more than anything in the world. He listened numbly
while she went on. 'Also, I should be very happy to know that
Jean was with you, for his own sake. He is not the sort of boy
we are accustomed to, and I think he needs other care than we
are able to give him.'

'What do you mean?' Hilary asked.

The nun seemed at a loss to know how to explain. 'Well,
he's a clever boy,' she said. 'Monsieur Mercatel thinks very
highly of him – he will have told you that himself. But one
can see that he's clever in a different way from the other
boys, and it is not a way that will help him in the careers we
have to offer. As I think I told you, our best boys are trained
for a good trade, and for most of them it's a better life than
they have any right to expect. But little Jean – he's not clever
in that kind of way. One would rather expect him to be a
schoolmaster or – or a writer like yourself, monsieur,' she
finished in relief.

Hilary argued, 'But if he stays with you, is there no future
for him but to learn a trade? Don't any of your boys get
adopted, for instance?'

The nun smiled wryly. 'Yes,' she said, 'some of our boys
occasionally are adopted by the local farmers who are looking
for labour when their own sons have left the farms for the

cities. But what farmer is going to adopt a puny child like that?'

Unexpectedly Hilary felt himself flooded with rage. He's not puny, he cried to himself, he's thin, maybe, but anyone can see he's worth a hundred of the other husky louts; and anyway, even if he is puny, whose fault is that? But the Mother Superior was speaking again.

'I will be frank with you, monsieur,' she said, 'I have my responsibilities, not only to this child, but to the orphanage as a whole. As I told you, we are a very poor foundation and we depend wholly on charity. Our rule is that each child must be recommended to us by a parent, a relation or a patron who is prepared to bear some part, no matter how small, of the cost of maintenance. We do not regret taking little Jean, nor do I think I was wrong to do so. But I cannot hide from myself that by keeping him I am depriving some other child who has a better right to be here, and therefore if I see that Jean has a chance of a good home, and a home where he may continue in his religion, I should be failing in my duty if I did not try to avail myself of this chance.'

Hilary was shocked. He was shocked that charity should be weighed in the balance, he was shocked that the Mother Superior was prepared so coolly to relinquish a child that he irrationally felt should have had a special hold on her affections. He found he wanted to reproach her bitterly, to hurl at her the nose-picking, the forgotten birthdays, the walks that never went in the direction of the trains. He wanted to accuse her of lack of proper feeling such as a nun, a nun who had charge of orphan children, should be expected to display.

178

He said, 'That is very reasonable, ma mère. When do you want me to decide?'

She said hesitantly, 'I had hoped that you might have become fond of the child –' The sentence trailed off and Hilary ignored it. He said, 'I will let you know on Monday.' Why Monday, he wondered, but he repeated more firmly, 'Yes, I will let you have a definite decision on Monday,' then he rose, shook hands with her and went away.

* * *

So that's that, said Hilary as he walked down the hill; everything cut and dried, everything decided and bang goes my life.

It's no good thinking about that any more, he said. There's no longer any choice. I had better be practical.

I suppose I said Monday so as to leave myself some illusion of choice. On Monday I shall have been here a week; on Monday, I can reasonably take a decision.

All right, then, on Monday I will take Jean for his walk and I will tell him. (What shall I tell him, he wondered, what will he say?) Then I will tell the Mother Superior I have decided to take the child. She is a polite woman; she will acquiesce in the convention that it is my own decision.

It will be too late to take him away that night. (What will he think as he lies for the last time in the hard iron bed?) In the morning I will go and fetch him and take him in the train to Paris. (How excited he'll be to go in a train!) I will take him to an hotel. I will find Pierre. Everything will be all right again between Pierre and me.

That will be Tuesday. On Wednesday I will go to the Embassy. There will be formalities; the child will have to be put on my passport. All this may take some time. I better not reckon to leave for England before Friday.

There is the question of money. I suppose I should find out how much I owe at the hotel.

Ought I to buy him some clothes before we go?

I'll have to take him to the flat. I'll have to ring up Joyce. Perhaps Joyce would take him right away. If I marry Joyce I needn't take him to my mother, not until he and I are safe.

If I let myself become sentimental I could imagine his face when I told him, could imagine holding him tightly in my arms, telling him that his father had come at last to take him away and never let him go again. I could imagine taking him to the Zoo, buying him toys, tucking him up at night – Oh, God, he cried, I am not sentimental, I must be practical. On Monday I shall tell him, on Tuesday I shall take him to Paris – and then, with explosive relief – and at least I shall be out of this lonely dreary town.

The thunderstorm had still not broken when he reached the hotel.

* * *

For the first time since the day he had arrived, Hilary stopped again outside the glassed-in box in the hall.

'Madame,' he said, 'will you please make out my bill up to the present and let me have it tonight?'

The blue eyes snapped eagerly and inquisitively, 'Monsieur is leaving us?' she demanded.

'Not immediately,' said Hilary coldly, 'but I have been here for some time now, and naturally I wish to know how I stand.'

'Very well,' she said, matching his coldness, and he could feel the hard eyes following him as he went across the hall into the café.

There he sat with a cognac reading his detective story. It was written in a strange kind of slang, the French equivalent, he imagined, of Damon Runyon, and he was able to read it slowly, pausing to translate each paragraph into the appropriate American. He took no notice of the few townsfolk who occasionally came into or left the café, only sat bent over his book, wishing that the storm would break and clear this heaviness out of the air.

Suddenly he was assailed by the intolerable need he had known last night in the cinema. He saw again the flickering screen, heard the raucous unintelligible voices, smelt the cheap insidious perfume – yes, surely he really smelt the perfume? He looked up sharply and saw that a woman was standing beside his table.

He saw the large breasts swelling the low-buttoned white blouse; he saw the bright gold hair, the wet mouth, the brown desirous eyes. He had the illusion of recognition as he stared at her.

She said, 'I was asked to bring monsieur his bill.' He still stared at her without speaking and she added, 'Surely monsieur is the Englishman who asked for his bill?'

Slowly Hilary understood what she was saying. He rose to his feet and said, 'You must forgive my stupidity and surprise,

madame – I think I was half asleep. I had a feeling that I'd met you before.'

She shook her head. 'I've only just arrived,' she explained. 'I am the niece of Madame Leblanc. Sometimes I come from Paris to visit my aunt for the week-ends.'

'I am Hilary Wainwright,' he said. 'May I ask your name?'

'Nelly,' she answered, and smiled into his eyes.

He asked, 'Nelly, will you do me the honour of taking a drink with me?'

'It would have been perfect,' she said regretfully, 'but to-night, alas, it is impossible. My uncle and aunt are waiting for me to come back.'

Her remembered perfume and his remembered need were one. 'Tomorrow, then,' he demanded harshly.

'That might be arranged,' she conceded. She looked quickly behind her and said, 'I must go now or they will be coming to look for me. Au revoir.' She held out her hand and as he grasped it he felt her fingers fluttering over his palm. He sighed deeply. Then she took her hand away and went swiftly out of the room, and as the door shut, its bang was echoed by the first crash of the approaching storm.

CHAPTER THIRTEEN

Saturday

The next morning, when he remembered to look at the hotel bill, Hilary was appalled.

The high price he had originally been quoted seemed to bear no relation to the outrageous total. Everything he had eaten since he arrived now appeared to have been an extra, and all had been rated at prices far beyond reason. Yet there was, he realised, nothing he could do about it. Wishing to conceal, even from himself, that he was eating differently from the regular hotel fare, he had accepted each succulent suggestion that had been made to him and deliberately refrained from asking the price.

Now, with a pencil and paper, he tried to figure out his resources. At last he reckoned that by Monday he would have just enough to return to Paris with Jean and frugally pass the few days that must elapse before they could leave for England.

Then he said, What a fool I am! Once I get to Paris, Pierre will fix me up. There's nothing really to worry about. So I needn't cut off my steaks and my cognacs, he thought with shamefaced relief; I can see this through comfortably here

and then once I get to Paris I shall be all right, and he got up and dressed and went down to breakfast.

That morning he found it difficult to keep his eyes on his book. He was forever lifting them to glance hurriedly round the room, to be sure that he should notice if someone passed through. But there was only Mariette bustling to and fro, and now and again the *patron* shuffling hopefully in from the kitchen and then going away defeated, as each time Hilary instantly and defensively dropped his eyes to the print again.

The day was clear after the storm and to go for a walk in the cool frosty air was the obvious thing to do. But Hilary kept making excuses to himself. I ought to get on with my article, he told himself. I won't get much chance after I've got Jean to cope with. It's no use writing in my room; it only stops Mariette from getting on with the cleaning. I'd better take my note-book into the café where I shall get some peace.

She came in after he had been waiting there for half an hour, pretending to write. The café was empty except for themselves. He leapt to his feet and said, 'Good morning, madame. May I offer you that drink now?'

'Why, I was really looking for Lucien,' she said, not troubling to make the excuse sound credible, 'No, I can't accept your offer now. If you're really serious –' She leant against the bar, frankly offering her body to his eyes.

'I'm really serious,' he said. 'When?'

'Meet me this evening at half-past eight, by the second lamp-post round the corner,' she said, and he had the impression that this glib assignation had been offered before. 'I'll be there,' he said, and she went quickly out of the café, pausing at

the door to smile at him over her shoulder, and now, as there was no need to pretend any more, he went out and walked round the town.

* * *

That evening, walking down the hill with the little boy, Hilary felt himself filled with a sense of absolute power. It was as it had been when, in his childhood, he had been given a secret to keep and had known that at some given moment he would be able to disclose it and then would be, for that instant, the source of absolute benevolence. Not for worlds would he have revealed himself before the given time for now, in the waiting, he was tasting a sensation almost forgotten and yet infinitely delightful.

And so, with the intensifying of his reactions, the day's meeting was gayer, livelier, more animated than any day before. They talked of Africa, and Hilary told Jean of the singing stones of Memnon, of the crocodiles that come when the black people call to them, of forgotten Roman cities suddenly discovered in a wilderness of sand. They talked of trains and Hilary was telling about the trans-Siberian express that took a fortnight to run from Harbin to Moscow, about sleeping-cars and restaurant-cars and about funiculars and cable-railways. They talked of Hilary's childhood and the toys he had had in his nursery – the rocking horse, the tricycle, the roller-skates and the wigwam – for surely there was no reason now to refrain from talking of those things? He could forget to be careful and watchful. For the first time since he had left Lisa in Paris, he was enjoying himself without contrasting his

present pleasure with his past and future misery. 'I had a lion that walked along when you wound him up,' he told the boy. 'I used to make him walk outside the wigwam and shoot at him with my bow and arrows. If I hit him, I used to bandage him up and pretend he became tame and friendly because he was so glad I'd helped him.'

The boy started as if he suddenly remembered something. He laid his red gloves carefully on the table and began fumbling under his overall.

Hilary broke off. 'What is it, Jean?' he asked.

'I've got a toy, too,' said Jean. 'Would you like to see it?'

'I'd love to,' said Hilary, and after frantic searches in a ragged pocket the boy at last pulled out the little bandaged headless swan that Hilary had last seen tumbled among the guilty pile on the grey blanket.

'This is my toy,' he said promptly, and his eyes searched Hilary's face.

Hilary's first impulse was to say quickly, I'll get you a better toy than that. Then he realised with surprise that the motive that restrained him was simply politeness. How queer, he thought, that I must let politeness, such as I would offer to another adult, take precedence over my natural wish to give.

He had waited too long. The boy's hand closed over his rejected toy. Hilary watched his lip tremble, and then, with great respect, heard him say, 'I like him, anyway.'

'So do I,' said Hilary quickly. 'He's just like the one I used to have in my bath.'

'Is he really?' asked Jean doubtfully. He took his hand off

the battered swan and looked at it critically. 'Did yours have his head off too?' he asked.

'Yes, he did,' lied Hilary, 'but I loved him just as much.'

Jean smiled tenderly. 'I love my swan better than anybody in the world, except Robert,' he said.

'Is Robert very nice to you?' Hilary asked.

'Quite nice,' said Jean judicially. He seemed to be thinking hard and then he added, 'Robert said I loved him best in the world.'

'Oh, I see,' said Hilary, relieved, yet oddly jealous of the reciprocal love Robert must himself have offered.

The boy added, 'Sister Clothilde took my swan away but Robert got it out of the cupboard and gave it back to me.'

Hilary realised that with this confidence he had been ranged on the side of Jean's protectors. Struck by a thought he asked, 'Do you love Sister Thérèse and Sister – what was her name? – Sister Clothilde?'

'No,' said Jean without interest, pushing the swan to and fro across the table.

'Do you love anyone at the orphanage?' Hilary pursued.

'I don't think so,' said Jean, still intent on the swan.

Hilary wanted to ask, Do you love me? but dared not. How nice it would be if he did, he thought suddenly, and the sentimental fancies he tried so hard to banish came flooding back into his mind, the thin arms clasped round his neck, the pale cold face pressed against his – and then he thought of other arms and another face and said sharply, 'Well, put the swan away safely. It's time to go home.'

* * *

He had waited a long time under the second lamp-post round the corner before she came. 'I couldn't get away before,' she said, taking his arm and pressing close to his side, 'and it wouldn't have done if I'd got here first. What would people have thought if they'd seen me waiting in the street?' and she laughed, shaking her hair so that it brushed his shoulder and he smelt again the cheap insidious perfume.

'Is there anywhere particular you'd like to go?' he asked, while his hand slid down her arm and clasped her wrist.

She shrugged her shoulders. 'Usually I go to Dupont's café,' she said, 'it's the best there is in this morgue of a town.'

'Then let's go there,' Hilary agreed, and she led him through back streets till they emerged at the bomb-shattered town-centre and began to cross it.

To cover his growing excitement Hilary asked politely, 'Do you often come down here?'

'I come about once a month,' she answered. 'I live in Paris, you see, and I can get hold of things that are difficult here – cigarettes and coffee and so on. My aunt is always glad to have them, and in exchange she gives me cheese and butter and eggs which in Paris are quite impossible, and so I don't manage so badly.'

Again Hilary was repelled by the open avowal of corruption, but this time his repulsion was fuel to his desire. The more corrupt he could find this woman, the more would her attraction for him grow. 'What do you do in Paris?' he asked.

'I've got a hat-shop on the Boulevard Malsherbes,' she said. 'It's called Nelly, right across the window in gold, just like

handwriting. I've got a very chic clientèle. Perhaps you'd like to come and buy one of my hats for your wife?' and he felt her pull on his arm so that she could try to see his face in the moonlight.

But he ignored her question and asked instead, 'Is your name really Nelly?'

'I was christened Eulalie,' she said with a loud laugh, 'but when I went into business, I had to choose something else. And American names are so chic, don't you think?'

'It suits you,' he agreed and then they came to the café in the new part of the town, just the sort of place she would choose, thought Hilary, shining mock mahogany and chromium plate, a radio blaring in the corner and a bunch of young men in purple suits and spotted bow-ties, who greeted Nelly with something more than the familiarity of old acquaintances.

This was the atmosphere Hilary most loathed, and yet again his loathing for the place and the people she had brought him to made him desire Nelly still more. The more cheap and vulgar, the more blatantly a sexual animal she could appear, the more certain he became that this was the object on which he could spend passion without emotion. He watched her with contemptuous delight while she drank his brandy and talked to the young men about the bicycle-races that would be passing through A—— next week. The chatter flared around him while he thought of the queer change that Parisian women undergo between the delicate faun-like beauty of their youth and the predatory brassiness of their middle-age and how seldom it was that one saw, as he

could see in Nelly, the brief stage of transition between the two.

She remembered him and said, 'You're being very quiet, aren't you? Monsieur is an Englishman,' she said proudly to the circle around her.

'Your first Englishman, Nelly?' one of them asked slyly.

'What a question!' she said, and went off into a roar of laughter that set her big breasts quivering under her satin blouse.

Hilary stood up and said, 'Let's go, Nelly.'

'Already?' she said, pouting, and then she looked sideways into his face and said, 'All right, let's go. Good night, every-one.'

'You going to the circus tomorrow?' someone called, as they went to the door.

Circus! thought Hilary delightedly, then I can take Jean to the circus! Nelly said provocatively, 'Well, I might go if I can find anyone to take me,' and followed by a chorus of ribald invitations they left the café.

Nelly pulled her coat around her and said, 'We'd better be getting back or they'll be wondering where I am.'

Hilary said, 'Does it matter?'

'Yes,' said Nelly, 'it does. You see, my husband's still a prisoner-of-war – God knows when he'll get back – and if my aunt finds out anything about me, then she'd probably tell him and he might stop my allowance.'

'So you're married,' said Hilary.

She shrugged her shoulders, 'He's been away for more than five years now,' she said. 'One must lead a normal life.'

Hilary was silent, and she tugged at his arm to make him look at her, adding anxiously, 'You mustn't think I'm not particular. Take the Boches, for instance – they offered me everything you can think of, but I wouldn't do it. No, I said, I'm not the type that sleeps with Germans, and you can believe me, I never did.'

She's lying, thought Hilary, with a kind of exultant delight. She's slept with Germans, the dirty bitch, and with anyone else who had enough to offer. They were passing the bombed church now and suddenly he dragged her into the shadow of its empty doorway, pushing her against the hard stone as he pressed his body to hers, his tongue between her lips, draining with thirsty relief the warm comfort of her mouth.

At last he took his mouth away and sighed, almost grunted with deep satisfaction. Slowly he passed his hands over her body while she shivered under his touch. Then he kissed her again, deeply and with desperation, and she clung to him, telling him with her body that her desire matched his own.

He lifted his mouth to whisper hoarsely, 'Let's go back. You can come to my room.'

She put a hand up and stroked his cheek. She murmured, 'I can't,' pressing her body against his as she said it.

He pushed her hand away and held it down to her side, 'Why can't you?' he demanded, 'I want you. You must.'

'You mustn't be unkind to me,' she said, her mouth close to his, so that he could smell her warm sickly-sweet breath, 'You know I want to. But I sleep next to my aunt

and she'd hear if I went. You can't imagine how she watches me.'

Hilary said, 'But I must have you.' He looked behind him to the cavernous depths of the ruined church and turned to her again, whispering, 'Why not here? Now?'

She jerked herself away from him. 'How can you suggest such a thing?' she cried with outraged pride. 'Do you think I'm a gipsy?'

'But I want you,' Hilary insisted despairingly; 'Don't you want me?'

'It wouldn't be proper,' she said. She added with mounting anger, 'And in a church, too! What kind of a woman do you take me for?'

So she wants to pretend, thought Hilary wearily. She wants me to mime the flattery, the respect, the devotion, the whole simulacrum of love. She refuses to act in my comedy: I must play the buffoon in hers.

Suddenly he felt exhausted and walked away from her to lean his forehead on the cold stone of the wall, wishing only to be alone and asleep, beyond decision or memory.

She called after him with a note of anxiety, 'Will you take me to the circus tomorrow?'

'What?' he said. Wearily he straightened himself and slowly walked back to her. 'What did you say?'

She repeated nervously. 'Will you take me to the circus tomorrow?'

'Take *you*?' he said, 'take *you*?' He began to laugh without any humour. 'What time is this circus tomorrow?' he asked.

'There's a performance at three,' she said quickly, 'but I

can't manage that because I've got to go out with Aunt. Then there's the second one at half-past seven. I could get away for that all right, and we could go to the funfair afterwards, and you could win some prizes for me. I'm sure you're good at shooting. All Englishmen are. Do say you'll take me?' She moved close to him, turning up her face to his and smiling invitingly into his eyes.

But he wasn't thinking of her. 'So there's a funfair too,' he said, thoughtfully.

'Yes, of course,' she said. She was growing impatient. 'Well,' she asked, 'are you going to take me or aren't you?'

What a pity there isn't a programme about six, he was thinking, and then he became conscious of Nelly again. 'Yes, of course. I'd love to take you,' he said hurriedly, 'but I'm afraid I couldn't get away by half-past seven.'

'Well, if you don't want to,' she said, 'I can easily find someone else who'd be glad to come with me,' and she turned her back on him, took a lipstick out of her bag and began smearing it on to her lips.

'Nelly,' he pleaded, 'I do really want to take you. The thing is, there's a child I have to go and see up at the orphanage – the child of an old friend of mine. I don't get away from him until half-past seven.'

She said coldly, 'Surely you could get rid of the kid a bit earlier – if you really wanted to, that is,' and she snapped her lipstick back into its case and started to walk away.

He caught her up, grasped her shoulders and swung her round to face him. 'All right,' he promised angrily, 'I'll meet you there at half-past seven. Where is it?' She told him, and

while he walked beside her, incoherent with anger and thwarted desire, a part of his mind was thinking, 'No, it's not too far to take Jean with me, first.'

CHAPTER FOURTEEN

Sunday

So the next afternoon Hilary took Jean to the fair.

It had occurred to him earlier that he might have asked to take the boy in time for the afternoon performance, to-day being Sunday and surely no lessons to be done. Then he thought, no, I'm not that fond of circuses, I couldn't stick it twice in one day. After all, he doesn't know about it, and the funfair by itself will be an unprecedented treat. There'll be plenty of time for circuses later on, Bertram Mills circus, the Royal Tournament, Madame Tussaud, and the pantomime – 'Look, Daddy look!' – the hot little hand clutching his coat, the big eyes radiant with excitement. Yes, there would be plenty of time later on.

'We're not going to look at trains this afternoon,' he said as they came down the steps, and then quickly, as Jean's eyes widened into the despairing stare that lacerated him, 'We're going to do something much more thrilling.'

'What is it, monsieur?' begged Jean, and Hilary said, 'You wait and see. It's something quite wonderful, but –' he remembered – 'we'll have to be quick if we are to have enough

time,' and he took the boy's hand in his and began to stride
quickly towards the plot of waste ground on the outskirts
where the circus was pitched.

The circus was a much grander affair than Hilary had
anticipated. The tent in the middle seemed gigantic and
around it were clustered caravans, booths, swings, wheels, all
the panoply of the fair. 'Oh, what is it?' begged Jean as they
came towards it and the noise of the clanking brassy music
and the excited crowds swelled to a roar.

'It's a circus,' said Hilary proudly, and 'A circus!' repeated
the boy, and ran beside Hilary, his pale face entranced.

'Shall we go and see the animals?' Hilary suggested, and
the boy nodded, mute with wonder. They went first into the
tent where the horses were stabled, tiny little coal-black
Shetland ponies, huge flat-backed piebalds, white horses with
flowing manes and tails, pale Arabs pointed with black, and
all the while Jean clutched Hilary's hand and said nothing,
drowned in wondering rapture.

Then they went to see the monkeys and the lions, and
lastly the solitary elephant who was accepting coins from the
spectators and handing them dutifully to his keeper. They
stood watching for a few minutes and then suddenly Jean let
go of Hilary's hand and stepped forward. Hilary, too startled
to move, watched Jean pull from his pocket the crumpled
red gloves and place them in the elephant's groping nostrils,
watched the elephant uncertainly wave the surprising offering in the air and then deposit it, like the others, in his
keeper's hand.

Hilary stepped quickly forward and caught hold of the

boy's shoulder, 'Why did you do that?' he demanded, and Jean said in bewilderment, 'I don't know. I wanted to give him something. He is so – so –' and broke off, at a loss for words.

The keeper had come up to them and was offering to give the gloves back. 'Look, Jean,' said Hilary, 'don't you want to take your red gloves?' but the little boy pressed close to Hilary and shook his head. 'I want the elephant to have them,' he said, and tried to drag Hilary away from the tempting sight of the proffered bundle.

That's like Lisa, Hilary thought instinctively, letting himself be pulled away from the elephant, and then wondered in surprise why he had thought it. It was not the gesture itself, not the simple act of generosity; rather it was the element of propitiation in it, the offering of all one held most dear in order to be allowed to retain happiness. Lisa, he remembered now, had always been afraid of happiness, had always envisaged jealous gods waiting to snatch it away. Then he told himself that he was making too much of the child's action, that there was no more in it than a simple admirable wish to give.

'Let's see if we can win some prizes,' he suggested, and they stopped at a booth where little balls could roll down a board into numbered holes.

They had several tries at this, several times getting their money back but winning no prizes. Then they threw coins on to a marked sheet and here Jean won a hideous enamelled ashtray. They stopped by a man who was spinning balls of coloured sugar, a teaspoonful of sugar swiftly spun into feathery tendrils that wreathed themselves round a wooden

197

stick and clung like a woolly mop to the end of it. Jean licked
at his with enthusiasm and Hilary a little shamefacedly
bought a second for himself and licked the stick as clean as
Jean's. Then Hilary threw darts and won a wooden spoon and
then he bought Jean a huge red balloon and gradually they
moved on to the swings and roundabouts.

Hilary decided against the swings. As a child he had
himself often been sick after swings and he wanted to run no
risks. 'We'll go in the bumpy-cars,' he said, and climbed into
a bright blue car and set the boy beside him.

Jean liked the bumpy-cars. His trophies piled on the seat
between them, he clung to the sides like grim death, shrieking
in uncontrolled excitement every time another car crashed
into them. He's a game little chap, Hilary thought, and after
they had had three goes on the bumpy-cars, he suggested,
'What about looking for a roundabout?'

Holding Jean's hand tightly lest he lost him in the noisy
milling crowds Hilary looked for a roundabout. They soon
passed a little one operated by hand where children about
Jean's age sat frigid with wonder in motor-cars and motor-
cycles with high safe sides. Hilary felt Jean tugging hopefully
at his hand, but he, too, wanted to share the pleasure and
he dragged him towards the biggest roundabout of all. As
roundabouts went, this one was peerless. It had been newly
painted, and Generals Leclerc, Montgomery, Zhukov and
Eisenhower beamed all round its canopy. Its twisted barley-
sugar rods shone like gold, and all around on the dais
pranced shiny horses and ostriches and lions and swans.
'We'll go on a swan,' said Hilary with pleasure, 'Up you go,'

and he hoisted the boy up on to the swan's back and climbed up behind him.

The machinery clanked, the music ground up, and faster and faster swirled the swan. Then Hilary felt the boy tremble in his encircling arm, felt him shake convulsively and at last heard his thin terrified screams above the blaring music. 'I want to get off,' he was crying, 'I want to get off.'

Hilary was frightened lest the boy's frenzied movements should indeed throw them off the hurtling swan which was now rising and falling with frantic velocity. 'Keep still, you little fool,' he hissed, 'be quiet, can't you?' but nothing could quiet the now hysterical child and Hilary, desperately concentrating on holding them both on, felt his anger rising and ever more furiously whispered, 'Shut up, can't you, shut up!'

At last the roundabout creaked to a standstill, and now Hilary's problem was to release the child's fingers from their convulsive clasp round the swan's neck. 'Let go, Jean,' he muttered frantically, increasingly conscious of the interested faces on the ground below, and in the end the boy's fingers grew limp and he let himself be pulled off.

As he climbed down to the ground, the boy awkwardly tucked under his arm, a middle-aged woman said angrily to him, 'You ought to know better than to take such a baby on a thing like that.' He pushed past her, numb with embarrassment, and at last set the boy down in a secluded corner between two caravans.

Then they looked at each other in dismay, the boy still whimpering, dirty tears splashed all over his face.

Hilary said nothing. He stood there watching the child, feeling only hate for the creature who had put him in this predicament, through whose intervention he had made a fool of himself. The little coward, he was saying, the little coward.

Jean whimpered, 'I want my red gloves back.'

You're finding out you can't buy happiness, thought Hilary coldly. Aloud he said, 'You can't have them back. Once you've given a present, it's a present for ever.'

Jean stopped whimpering, only stood there shaking and staring. You're finding out what desolation means, thought Hilary savagely, all right, I had to; but underneath his anger was a curious delight in knowing that the greater the boy's misery now, the greater would be the comfort he had ultimately to offer.

'I've lost my balloon,' said Jean in a voice drained of all hope.

'I'll get you another balloon,' said Hilary impatiently, and he seized the child's hand and dragged him towards a balloon-seller. 'There!' he said, proffering the gift with what he knew to be unacceptable unkindness, and watched without surprise while the child let the string fall out of his hand and the balloon drop on to the ground and be instantly trampled upon.

What a swine I'm being, he thought; let me start again and restore him to happiness. 'Let's go and try that shooting-place over there,' he said in a carefully neutral voice, pointing to a gaudy booth a little way away, and Jean, in a voice as expressionless as his own said, 'Yes, let's go and try it.'

But Hilary suddenly remembered to look at his watch and it was already seven o'clock; quarter of an hour back to the orphanage, quarter of an hour back to the circus again. 'No, we

can't,' he said roughly, 'we've got to be getting back, or I'll be late.'

Now Jean was any whining child, dragging at his hand. 'Oh, monsieur,' he whimpered, 'I do want to go to that shooting-place. Please can't we go to the shooting-place?'

'No, we can't,' said Hilary. With horror he heard himself saying, 'I bring you down here and give you a treat, and look at the way you behave.' So this is what paternity does to you, he thought in furious shame, and he strode to the road, the whining child running to keep up with him.

'Can't you hurry?' he kept on urging, as they pressed on up the hill. 'Can't you walk a bit faster?' and Jean would reply in the now detestable whine, 'I can't hurry. I'm too tired,' and drag ever more heavily on Hilary's hand. 'All right, I'll carry you,' Hilary said at last, and he picked up the little boy and held him in his arms as he had so often longed to hold him, and there the little boy fell asleep, tired out with excitement and misery and loss.

Gradually the slight weight seemed heavier and heavier and he trudged ever more slowly up the hill. And as he walked, his anger against the boy died away and he was left only with his anger against himself which must either be expiated or must consume him utterly.

The boy opened his eyes as Hilary climbed up the orphanage steps and in the light reflected from the transom Hilary saw him smile like any happy child awakened from sleep to an assurance of happiness. Without knowing what he was going to do he bent his head and kissed the child's pale cold cheek and then quickly put him down, pushed him inside the door, and went away.

CHAPTER FIFTEEN

Sunday – continued

He caught up with Nelly as she was walking to the entrance of the circus tent where they had arranged to meet. 'So you managed to get rid of the kid all right,' she said, 'seems funny, you taking all that trouble over somebody else's brat. One wouldn't have said you were the type.'

'What type do I look?' Hilary demanded, pressing beside her into the huge dim tent. Now she knew all the answers, could flutter her lashes and reply coquettishly, 'You look much too fierce and dangerous to be left with children. Why, I'm quite frightened of you myself,' and Hilary laughed shortly and followed her into the expensive ringside seats that he knew she would expect as her due.

She settled into the red plush with studied and voluptuous content but Hilary, watching her face, was surprised to see it beaming with just the unsophisticated delight of the local girls all around. 'I do love a circus,' she said, squeezing his hand, but not forgetting, even then, the automatic flutter of the fingers, and then, 'Oh, look, they're going to begin.'

The conductor raised his baton, the tent flaps were pulled

aside, and the circus had begun. Hilary watched without interest, grimacing politely whenever Nelly turned her delighted face to his, but secretly resentful of her simple enjoyment. Whenever the clowns tumbled in the sawdust, when the sides of the property car fell off, when water was splashed unrestrainedly over everyone in the ring, Nelly sat shaking in her seat, hooting with exuberant gulps of laughter. Hilary was angry at her crude bucolic sense of fun, wanting her vicious, bored, sophisticated, finding nothing to desire in the heavy thighs flattened against the seat, the breasts that wobbled with each burst of merriment.

Then, in the second half of the programme, the ring-master announced, 'Monsieur Stefanov and his World-Famous Dancing Horse!' There was a long low roll of drums, and then the orchestra broke into the Blue Danube and the dancing horse waltzed into the ring. His coat was of a golden colour, polished till it gleamed like metal, and over his hindquarters the hair had been combed into a checkerboard pattern that caught and reflected the light as he twisted and curvetted. He danced a waltz and a polka and a tango, and his body and the movements of his body were of such grace and beauty that Hilary was entranced. He watched the golden horse with absorbed intensity, translated into ecstasy as long as those exquisite movements were deployed before him.

When it was over and the dancing horse had gone, to be replaced by a funny man on a tight-rope, Hilary's feelings had undergone a complete change. In the ecstasy induced by beauty, all around him was transformed, and Nelly, shaking with merriment beside him, was the desirable object

on which his exaltation could find fulfilment. She was again the warm infinitely desirable creature who could promise satisfaction and comfort beyond unsatisfying thought, and he pressed close to her in the dark, surrendering himself to the mounting urgency of desire.

They came out into the dark flare-lit fairground and Nelly said, 'I'm hungry. Let's find some food here and then you can win some prizes for me.' 'All right,' Hilary agreed, and they pushed their way to a refreshment booth, plates of cut meats set out on its counter, and some small tables on the grass.

Hilary fetched plates of food and some beer and sat facing Nelly across one of the tables. 'Did you get away without your aunt knowing?' he asked, and she said, 'I told her I was going to visit an old friend. Not that she believed me – she's an old cow, that one – but there wasn't anything she could do about it.'

Hilary said, 'Couldn't we go back late and then you could come to my room on your way up without her knowing?'

'I'm not taking any chances,' said Nelly, 'and anyway,' she added with professional hauteur, 'you're taking a lot for granted, aren't you?'

'Am I?' said Hilary, and he reached across the table and laid his hand on hers, staring into her eyes.

She laughed, 'Perhaps not,' she said playfully and then she leant across the table and whispered, 'I was thinking about you all night, asking myself how things could be arranged. Now I have had a very good idea. Tomorrow I go back to Paris – why don't you come with me?'

'Tomorrow?' said Hilary, still staring at her. His grip slackened on her wrist.

'I'm going back on the last train,' she explained. 'I don't open my shop until Tuesday when I come here for the weekend. You and I could go up to Paris together and I think' – she pouted at him invitingly – 'we could manage to amuse ourselves without anyone to look on.'

Hilary said desperately, 'Tomorrow – tomorrow's horribly difficult for me. Couldn't I come and meet you on Tuesday?' I could put Jean in an hotel, he was thinking. I could tip the chambermaid to keep an eye on him, there'd be no harm –

'No, I couldn't manage Tuesday,' she said, and withdrew her hand.

'Then Wednesday – Thursday?' begged Hilary.

'None of those days,' she said decisively. She filled her mouth with food and began slowly chewing. When she had emptied it, she said, 'I'll tell you how things are. I've got a friend, you see – the one who financed my shop. He comes back from the country every Tuesday, and he doesn't expect me to make any dates for the rest of the week.'

That's how I wanted you, thought Hilary savagely, somebody else's kept woman, the ultimate degradation. *Je suis son paillard, ma paillarde me suit.* 'What does your boyfriend do?' he asked.

'He's a wholesale butcher,' she said. 'He's got plenty of money.' She fingered the gold bangle round her wrist. 'I've got a nice little flat,' she whispered insinuatingly, 'we'll go eating, we'll go dancing, and then we'll come back home, just you and me.' She waited for his response and then said to his silence, as she had said the night before, 'Of course, if you don't want to come –'

'Of course I want to come,' said Hilary frantically, 'of course I want to. You know that. It's only that I'm tied up with business, that I'm trying to think how I could arrange things. You know how much I want to come. What time does your train go?'

'Five thirty-five,' she said, looking at him eagerly. 'You'd have to meet me at the station – if I walk through the town with you in broad daylight, someone is sure to see us. And I don't suppose,' she added playfully, 'that you want that any more than I do.'

'No, I don't,' said Hilary, thinking of Madame Mercatel in her high-backed chair beside the fire. 'Isn't there a later train?' he asked, arguing, I could take him too, no, I couldn't do that, what could I do?

'That's the last one,' she said, 'trains aren't like what they were before the war. Well, are you coming or aren't you?'

'Let's go and have a look at the fair,' said Hilary suddenly, standing up, 'then I can think of ways and means – and I'll find a way.'

'I'm beginning to think you don't want to come,' she said over her shoulder as she walked out of the tent, and he caught her hand, dragged her round to the back and kissed her desperately. 'Now do you believe I want to come?' he whispered, bringing his mouth down again and again on hers, and she pressed herself into his body and whispered back, 'You must come, you must.'

Then they walked round the fair, arms entwined, throwing rings, rolling coins, stopping now and again in a patch of

darkness to kiss and caress and refuel their desire. It's either – or, thought Hilary as he made the automatic responses, performed the expected movements. If I go with her, it's the end. If I go with her, I shall have to spend on her all the money I've got left. If I go with her and spend all my money, I can't go to Pierre for more; I can never see Pierre again. If I go with her I must go back to England on Tuesday, back to the flat, back to barren security. If I go with her, I have already seen Jean for the last time.

Then, What nonsense, he said angrily. Of course it needn't be the end. Even if I go back to England, there's nothing to stop me coming back later, getting more foreign currency, perhaps next month, perhaps next year. But this month, this time, now, I can escape. He suddenly stopped and turned so that he faced her. He said breathlessly, 'I want you. I'll meet you at the station tomorrow.'

'I thought you would,' she said softly. She was confident that what she had to offer was stronger than any other desire could be. She smiled at him lasciviously and repeated, 'I thought you would.'

They stood still for a moment while the crowds swirled about them, she with eyes narrowed, calculating possibilities, he defiant, angry, certain only of overpowering desire. Then she caught his hand and said, 'Come on, let's have one more try at winning some prizes before we go back. Let's try this one,' she said, and she dragged him towards the shooting-booth where he had planned his reconciliation with Jean, whence he had turned Jean away to meet this woman who was now the sum of all his desires.

And there, facing him among the rows of prizes, sat a pink velvet dog with one ear up and one ear down, just such a pink velvet dog as had once sat waiting at a fair in Carpentras.

'It's Binkie!' he said with incredulous recognition.

'What are you looking at?' demanded Nelly shrilly. She followed his eyes, 'Oh, what a pretty little dog!' she simpered with an artificial laugh. 'Do win him for me.'

Hilary pushed forward, laid down his money, and picked up a gun. He chose his target, fired without thought or care, certain that he must win. 'I'll have the pink dog,' he said, and then, when the dog was handed over, turned away and stood bewildered, the ridiculous animal pressed to his breast.

Nelly snatched it from him. 'Isn't he sweet?' she exclaimed, rubbing her cheek on the velvet head. She relapsed into baby talk, making love to the dog, her eyes on Hilary.

'But you can't have him,' Hilary said, still bewildered. 'He's not for you.'

'Don't be silly,' she said in the same caressing voice. 'Why, I wouldn't give him up for anything.'

'I'll win you something else, something nicer.' Hilary pleaded. He pushed his way back to the stall, but he was shooting wildly now and he won no more prizes.

He dived into his pockets. 'Look!' he said, and brought out the wooden spoon and the enamel ashtray that he had thrust there for safety when he and Jean had climbed on to the round-about. 'Look,' he said, 'won't you change Binkie for these?'

She took his offerings and examined them critically.

'Where did you get these from?' she asked.

'I won them earlier,' he stammered, 'when – when I was waiting for you.'

Her eyes narrowed suspiciously. 'And what did you call the little dog – Beenkie, was it?'

He said desperately, 'We – I once had a toy dog like that – a long time ago. It was called Binkie. That's why I want this one.'

She was still distrustful. 'You're not going to give it to anyone else?' she demanded.

'No, of course not,' Hilary assured her, and at that moment he knew what he was going to do with the dog.

She tossed it to him. 'All right,' she said, 'baby can have his toy.' She slipped the ashtray into her handbag, dropped the wooden spoon on to the ground, saying contemptuously, 'That's no use to me.' They began to wander out of the fairground, back to the dark streets. She said in his ear, 'You'll have to get me something very nice in Paris to make up,' and he promised her wildly, 'I'll get you anything you want in Paris, anything, if you'll only be kind to me.'

'But of course I'll be kind to you,' she said soothingly, and her voice was warm and comforting. It was gratitude now, not passion, that made him stop and pull her closely to him. He was stroking her hair, kissing her with quick delicate kisses, murmuring words of fondness, not desire. He was rediscovering a range of familiar actions, and with them the old forgotten emotions. He groaned. 'What is it?' she asked, and he replied quickly, 'Nothing – only that I need you so much,' while his heart shuddered under the knowledge that not even in this relationship, in which he sought only escape, could he partake without tenderness.

CHAPTER SIXTEEN

Monday

On Monday morning Hilary sat in his bedroom writing a letter.

'*Ma mère,*' he wrote, '*I find myself unexpectedly called back to England on urgent business before I have been able to decide anything definite about the boy. You may rest assured that if I reach any final decision I will let you know immediately.*' (Shall I tell her to keep me informed about him? he wondered, but thought, no, that would mean giving her my address.) '*I am sending a present for the child which I hope you will allow him to accept. It only remains to thank you for the kindness and consideration you have shown me, and to regret that I must leave so hurriedly that I cannot convey my thanks in person.*' From his memory, he dredged up the correct letter-ending formula and signed his name. There's nothing final in that, he said, nothing to prevent my coming back later if I change my mind; nothing but the humiliation I could never endure of coming back to face the woman who will read this letter and know me for the coward I am. Once she has read this letter, I can never come back, but I can still pretend not to know this. For my

comfort I must tell myself that there is still a loophole, that I can come back later. I will not let myself believe that I am lying.

He rang for the maid.

'Mariette,' he said when she came, 'Will you do something for me?'

'Of course, monsieur,' she said, pleased and flattered.

He pointed to the clumsy newspaper-wrapped parcel he had made. 'There is a present there for the little boy at the orphanage,' he said, 'but unfortunately I can't take it up myself because, you see, my train goes at the very time that they let visitors come. Do you think you could take the parcel up to the orphanage for me with this letter and give them both to the Mother Superior?'

Her brow puckered. 'At what time must they be delivered at the orphanage, monsieur?' she asked.

'At half-past five,' Hilary said, 'That's most important. They've got to be there at exactly half-past five.'

'Monsieur, I don't want to be ungracious,' she said timidly, 'but would it do if Lucien took them? I don't know if madame would let me go out at that time – it is when the new guests usually arrive, you see.'

'I don't want Lucien to take them,' Hilary said petulantly. His eyes filled with tears and he entreated, 'Couldn't you possibly do it?'

She put out a hand as if to pat his shoulder, and then drew it back hurriedly, 'I'll do it myself,' she promised, 'at half-past five exactly they will be at the convent.' She added, 'I shall be sorry to see monsieur leave us. Everyone seems to be going

to-day. Mademoiselle Nelly, she also goes back to Paris this evening.'

Hilary felt a throb of excitement at the sound of the name. To cover it he pulled out his note-case and gave money to the old woman. 'It is most good of you,' he said gratefully, 'I know I can rely on you,' and she repeated, 'At half-past five, monsieur, they will be there.'

* * *

He did not see Nelly during the day, but their arrangements had all been made the night before, and just before five he left the hotel to walk to the station.

So that's all over, he was saying, as he turned out of the archway into the cobbled street, it's all over and I'm free again.

He saw a jumbled version of the pleasures ahead, food and lights and perfume and music and at last the warm bed, the mounting desire, the climax of orgasm. His flesh throbbed greedily. There are only the streets to walk through, he said, and I shall be with her, beside her.

And at last my intolerable need will be satisfied.

Oh, I deserve it, he cried, after all I've been through, remembering the interminable empty days, the long dragging evenings. I deserve my pleasure. Oh, God, the release to be out of this damnable town and know I need never go back.

Never go back?

It will be all right once I'm really away, he told himself, once I'm in the train beside her and the going is irrevocable and beyond my decision to change it. Here in this town I am still oppressed with all its remembered agonies. But soon,

soon I shall be able to slough them off, to think only of the pleasures ahead and the final comfort.

Comfort but never happiness. I am not capable of happiness. No miracle happened to let me face happiness.

So now you want a miracle, said his conscience from the emptiness of the bomb-shattered square. Once you wanted to triumph in the ordeal.

I'm through with ordeals, cried Hilary. I haven't enough courage. I must escape.

He tried to walk quickly, but his bag was heavy in his hand. I did think for a minute, he allowed, that there was a miracle. I thought that I recognised the child.

But of course that was nonsense. No reasonable man could have accepted it. All I dare accept are facts.

These are the facts. There was no proof that the child was mine. I didn't come here to adopt a child but to find my own. I didn't find him and so I may go freely to my pleasure, freely to my invulnerability and to my memories.

To all my memories?

If I had let myself succumb to tenderness, he argued, it would have been simple. I would have been torn to pieces by this child. I would have taken him and comforted him and never let him go. But I dared not give tenderness.

Memory whispered in Pierre's voice, 'Each gives what he can: what that is, is settled long before.'

You see, pleaded Hilary, I am incapable of giving. I dare not give and so I'm running away. I've finished with ordeals. I am fleeing to the anaesthesia of immediate comfort and absolute non-obligation.

Then he whispered, but I haven't escaped from obligation, Nelly has dragged from me the obligation of tenderness.

Tenderness to Nelly? he thought, and shuddered.

In one of the houses he was passing a clock struck the quarter.

But if I must give tenderness to Nelly, he said slowly, if there is no escape from tenderness after all – then I have other obligations than hers.

I have an obligation to Pierre. I owe him the love he gave me, the friendship that I betrayed. I owe him his expiation.

I can give tenderness to Nelly. What can I give to Pierre?

If I took the child I should be able to pay my debt to Pierre.

I've betrayed them all, he said – Pierre my friend, Madame Mercatel, my mother, the laundress and the nun. I have betrayed the child.

But I had no obligation to the child, he cried. He is not my son, I had no obligation – only that I hurt him because I had the right to comfort him, and now I am going away and he will never be comforted.

He is not my child. If I take a child that is not my own, I shall be betraying Lisa.

Hilary stopped dead. How strange, he thought, how unutterably strange. I am not even sure of that.

It was for Lisa's sake that I came to look for our child. But he is still lost, is lost for ever. Would she have wanted me to take this one?

He thought, If I could know what she would have said. If I imagine her face, if I imagine her voice answering my question, I shall know what I should do.

He looked up to the tangled tramway wires, hit by the beam of a single flickering street-light. 'Lisa,' he said aloud, 'what do you want me to do?'

He tried with all the intensity of his imagination to call up her face, to see it turned to his, to see the lips moving, to hear her voice, some tone of her voice that he would remember and recognise. He could imagine nothing, could see nothing but the light on the tramway wires.

He said with final horror, I have forgotten Lisa. If I stay or if I go, I shall never know which is the greater betrayal.

* * *

Then he whispered, I could give tenderness to Nelly.

I can give –

And then, with absolute certainty, 'I can give love. In my heart, this child is my son.'

PART FOUR
The Judgment

CHAPTER SEVENTEEN

The little boy was sitting on a hard bench in the hall. He had been sitting there for a long time now.

Some while ago an old woman had rung the bell, and when Sister Thérèse had come, the old woman had handed her a parcel and a letter. 'I'd promised I'd come earlier,' she had said, 'but I couldn't get away. I did my best.' Then the old woman had gone, Sister Thérèse had taken the parcel and letter into the Mother Superior and, coming back through the hall, had glanced at the little boy and commented in her harsh voice, 'Monsieur seems to be late to-day.' But all that was a long time ago, and still the little boy sat waiting.

The Mother Superior came into the hall. She sat down beside the little boy and put her arm around him and he was surprised and uneasy for she had never done such a thing before. He looked at her anxiously and saw that her eyes were wet and shining.

She said in a curious voice, 'Here is a present for you,' and from under the folds of her robe she brought out the untidy newspaper parcel and laid it on his knees.

He knew what to do with presents now, but his hands were

cold and clumsy and it took him a long time to work off the string and pull the paper away.

Hilary came through the door to hear the little boy's shout of passionate triumph:

'It's Binkie! It's Binkie come back!'

AFTERWORD

It has been suggested by two separate sources that Marghanita Laski's *Little Boy Lost* had its origin in a true story which took place some three hundred or so years ago in Northern England. During the Civil War the Swinburne family, always strongly Roman Catholic and among the Northumbrian gentry who supported the Royalist cause, secretly spirited away the three-year-old heir, subsequently Sir John Swinburne, the first baronet, to be given a Catholic education in a French monastery: the boy's father, also called John, had been killed during an argument in 1643.

According to Hodgson's *History of Northumberland* (1827), a Northumbrian gentleman of the Radclyffe family, accidentally visiting the monastery a few years later, recognised in the child's face certain features of the Swinburne family.

> On enquiring of the monks, – how he came there? the only answer they could give was, that he came from England . . . On questioning the boy himself, it was, however, found that he had been told that his name was Swinburne, which, with the account of his father's death, and his own mysterious disappearance

in Northumberland, induced the superior of the house
to permit him to return home: where, in an inquest
specially empannelled for that purpose, he identified
himself to be the son of John Swinburne and Anne
Blount, by the description he gave of the marks upon
a cat, and a punch-bowl, which were still in the house.

Descendants of Sir John live to this day at Capheaton,
the house in Northumberland that he built in 1668 which was
described by Pevsner as 'one of the most interesting houses of
its date and character in England.' There is no evidence that
Marghanita Laski herself knew the Swinburne family but she
was formidably well-read and may easily have come across
an account of Sir John's origins in Hodgson's *History*. It is
possible that this was the seed that inspired her, and that she
then transposed elements of the story to post-war France.

Yet why did Marghanita Laski choose this setting? Partly
it was because she 'loved France and most things French' (*The
Times* obituary, February 1988) – she and her husband were
married in Paris in 1937 and lived there for a year. But even
before the war she had had an intense personal involvement in
the crisis of continental Europe. She had been at Oxford and,
although not actively political, had made friends with many
intellectuals. Her family was Jewish and had rescued two
Jewish refugees, a boy and a girl, shortly before the outbreak
of war; Marghanita was already living away from home at this
time, but it was she who met the boy from a London station
when he first arrived in this country, and heard him sing 'Baa
Baa Black Sheep' – the only words of English he had been

taught by his mother, who was later killed. His plight cannot have been absent from her thoughts when she was writing *Little Boy Lost;* which is partly why little Jean in the novel 'walks straight into the reader's heart. He is, in one sense, every lost child of Europe,' as the novelist Elizabeth Bowen wrote in her review.

In the novel Marghanita Laski used France as one of many countries where the war brought society to a state of collapse. Hilary Wainwright is asked: '"What do you think of France now?"' and replies, '"I think it is horrible – horrible and desperately unhappy. I used to love and admire France more than any country I knew, but coming back to it now, I find it enveloped in a miasma of corruption."' The image of a deeply divided post-war France, still prostrate from its brutal invasion, is brilliantly and chillingly evoked in *Little Boy Lost*. Its dramatic capitulation in 1940, leading to the end of the Third Republic and the creation of a collaborationist regime in Vichy, is something with which it is still coming to terms even today, for the humiliations that were endured cut deep and long into the national psyche. Laski's sharp intelligence foretold how difficult the process of restoring French pride would be; yet she remained an optimist. As the *Daily Mail* reviewer wrote: the novel 'takes in its sweep, without ever halting the story, the whole tragedy of post-war corruption – yet still leaves one with faith.'

During the German occupation most of the population had been forced to reach a compromise, often on a daily basis, between collaboration at one extreme and resistance at the other. Beginning with Marcel Ophuls's film *The Sorrow and*

the Pity (1971) modern France has gradually been forced to confront the evidence that far more people had made corrupt choices than had previously been admitted. And even for those who did resist, minor acts such as getting hold of food and looking after relations and friends often required as much courage as the more dramatic exploits of sabotaging bridges or distributing pamphlets. It is the aftermath of this world in which *Little Boy Lost* is set. '"Don't you wonder, with every stranger you meet, what he did under the Occupation?"' Hilary asks his friend Pierre. He replies: '"Oh, yes, but automatically now and without caring about the answer. I'm tired with 'collaborationist' as a term of abuse; we each did under the Germans what we were capable of doing; what that was, was settled long before they arrived."'

In the book one of the characters says:

> To me, the most horrible thing is hearing everyone excusing themselves on the grounds that deceit was started against the Germans and has now become a habit. It would have been better to have been honest, even with Germans, than to end by deceiving each other and finally deceiving ourselves.

Marghanita Laski describes in detail the operation of the black market economy and how insidious is the corruption that flows from this. She is also unsparing in her depiction of the realities of the orphanage, where the tubercular patients are mixed with the non-tubercular ('if you knew more of Europe, monsieur, you would know that to run the risk

of being infected with tuberculosis in a home where you have a bed to sleep in and regular meals is today to have a fortunate childhood') and where rickets is accepted as inevitable for those children forced to remain beyond the age of six; food, toys and love for the children are all inadequate; the sisters' brusque manner in dealing with their charges is one of their methods of survival and is contrasted with Hilary's naiveté.

> Monsieur, you English do not begin to comprehend what Europe is like to-day. You find that conditions in France are bad – believe me, monsieur, we are in Paradise. You could not begin to believe what I have been told by our sisters who have been working in Germany, in Austria, in Poland. When I could weep for our own children, then I remember what I have been told of those others.

'By 1947,' writes Mark Mazower in his *Dark Continent: Europe's Twentieth Century,* 'there were some 50,000 orphans in Czechoslovakia. In Yugoslavia the estimate was closer to 280,000... In Holland, some 60,000 children required help . . . in Bucharest there were 30,000 homeless. The UN Relief and Rehabilitation Agency was caring for some 50,000 unaccompanied children in Germany alone, many of whom had forgotten who they were or where they came from.'

French orphans were observed by Marghanita Laski at first hand: her daughter clearly remembers holidays in post-war France including regular visits to orphanages and long

conversations with the nuns. To anyone who has visited the ubiquitous, overcrowded orphanages of Albania or Roumania after the collapse of Communism it would seem that nothing much has changed: *Little Boy Lost* evokes an identical contemporary scenario, in which the dislocation of war and civil disruption invariably results in children's suffering. The book may describe post-war France – but in 2001 it is only too easy to say it could be post-war anywhere.

The town, fifty miles outside Paris, where the orphanage is located, is identified by Marghanita Laski only as A——, one which contains nothing but ugliness, ruin and desolation. It had always been ugly, grossly damaged in the First World War and 'rebuilt with that haphazard disregard for appearance so characteristic of modern France.' Yet the people whom Hilary 'regarded as the most civilised in the world had led full satisfactory lives, eating with informed pleasure, arguing with informed logic, strolling up and down in the warm summer evenings, sitting at cafes, and watching the promenade pass by'; and therefore it seemed to him 'that bomb damage in a French town was a greater tragedy than elsewhere because here the way of life destroyed was in complete antithesis to all that bombs were trying to achieve.'

But *Little Boy Lost* is also a timeless novel about emotion, about love; it describes a man's search to find himself, to come to terms with his own sense of loss and to find the courage to love again in the full knowledge that this will open himself up to the renewed possibilities of pain; by forcing Hilary Wainwright, putative father of the lost child yet the one who is truly lost himself, to exert a positive choice, a shape is given

to his existence, one which had lost its meaning after the death of the wife whom he had loved so passionately. (The climate of existentialist ideas emerging after the occupation from French writers such as Sartre and Camus was one with which Marghanita Laski was likely to have been very familiar.)

As the poet Stevie Smith wrote: 'The poor, cold child, starved of love but most endearing, and the father who fears he cannot love, seem frozen in time; there is great depth of feeling in this story and an admirable simplicity of style.' The key themes of the book are courage under pressure, loyalty, the exercise of individual conscience and the importance of duty. Duty may nowadays be an old-fashioned word, its meaning hard to understand, but for Hilary, a sympathetic character even though not all his qualities are admirable, it is a guiding force: 'I know my duty,' he thinks, as he agonises over whether or not to accept the child without knowing for certain if it is his. 'I came here prepared to do my duty. If the child were mine, I'd take him; if he weren't, I'd leave him. It was to be as simple as that. There was to be no place for feeling in such a decision. Duty must still be the operative word, not feeling.' Nor should he take on the boy simply out of overwhelming pity; even if, as he says to the Mother Superior, '"Ma mere, you must forgive me. I have become unused to pity, these past years – and to-day it has over-whelmed me."'

Yet by this stage Hilary has developed an emotional bond with the child, and the reader wants him to scoop the boy up and take him to live with him, irrespective of whether or not he is the biological father. Hilary insists, however, that he must

be sure of his paternity – 'If I've got to give up my precarious peace, my tentative security, I've got to be sure.' But why? He is surely concerned with more than genetic inheritance – he has, after all, been assured that the child is exceptionally bright and must have come from a cultured family similar to his own; nor is the child physically unlike him; while the kind-hearted gesture of giving away his gloves to the elephant is reminiscent of how Lisa would have behaved with the 'element of propitiation in it, the offering of all one held dear in order to be allowed to retain happiness.'

But all this of course proves nothing. More probably, Hilary recognises his own selfishness – that he does not even know whether he wants him to be his son, that he might subsequently resent the boy and the inevitable disruption to his ordered life. His own bad relationship with his mother makes him uncertain about being a father himself. There is also a fear that if this is not his son then his own son is still lost and might even, one day, be found. He says he must be sure for Lisa's sake. 'It was my child she wanted me to save, our child, the child of our love. I have no duty to save a pitiable orphan who is nothing to do with me.' He feels that anything less than finding and cherishing his own child is a betrayal of Lisa and the memory of their perfect relationship. And he does not have the endurance to love again. 'The traitor emotions of love and tenderness and pity must stay dead in me. I could not endure them to live and then die again.'

The way Laski ultimately resolves this enables Hilary to find the courage in peacetime which bot Lisa and his friend

Pierre had already shown in their different ways in time of war. He had wanted to run away and return to England because, everything he felt passionately about having been brutally snatched from him, he has become inured to real feeling. He is too intelligent not to realise that the little boy is dangerously close to reawakening his sensitivity to love. And so he keeps fighting against exposing himself to the pain that, of course, so often accompanies love. 'How can I give now when I want so much to be given?' is his piercing *cri de coeur*.

At the end of the book Hilary seeks to escape his dilemma through a purely sexual relationship with Nelly, the Parisian niece of the hotel owner – 'at last my intolerable need will be satisfied'. Although Hilary is repelled by her open corruption, 'this time his repulsion was fuel to his desire. The more corrupt he could find this woman, the more would her attraction for him grow.' His realisation that 'not even in this relationship, in which he sought only escape, could he partake without tenderness' makes her an essential character as she helps him to understand the difference between lust and love and even to re-evaluate what he once considered his perfect relationship with Lisa.

Only in the final pages does Hilary come to understand himself, enabling Marghanita Laski to write one of the most poignant endings in twentieth century fiction – a perfect ending to a beautifully written book. The 1949 advertisements quoted the critic Daniel George as saying (on the radio) that he had 'been brought as near to tears as any printed matter has brought me since the death of Little Nell.' And the critic SPB Mais wrote: 'In many ways this is a blood-curdling

book. It moved me much *more* than *Dombey and Son*. For one thing it is much better written.'

Just after the publication of *Little Boy Lost* Marghanita Laski sold the film rights, but was 'furious and hurt' (according to the *Dictionary of National Biography*) when, four years later, it was turned into a musical starring Bing Crosby: the serious moral issues were inevitably devalued by a version that focused only on a father's search for his son. For the book is so much more than this; and nowadays a new generation of readers, one that has not been forced to deal with moral choices in extreme circumstances, has to try and answer the impossible question, 'What would I have done?' As Elizabeth Bowen observed in her review of 'this tender and magnificent story . . . to miss reading *Little Boy Lost* would be to by-pass a very searching, and revealing, human experience.'

Anne Sebba
Richmond, 2001